THE LEGACY SERIES

Series Titles

Where Are Your People From?
James B. De Monte

Self-Defense
Corey Mertes

Finding the Bones: Stories & A Novella
Nikki Kallio

Sometimes Creek
Steve Fox

The Plagues
Joe Baumann

The Clayfields
Elise Gregory

Kind of Blue
Christopher Chambers

Evangelina Everyday
Dawn Burns

Township
Jamie Lyn Smith

Responsible Adults
Patricia Ann McNair

Great Escapes from Detroit
Joseph O'Malley

Nothing to Lose
Kim Suhr

The Appointed Hour
Susanne Davis

WHERE ARE YOUR PEOPLE FROM?

a novel in stories

JAMES B. DE MONTE

Cornerstone Press
Stevens Point, Wisconsin

Cornerstone Press, Stevens Point, Wisconsin 54481
Copyright © 2023 James B. De Monte
www.uwsp.edu/cornerstone

Printed in the United States of America by
Point Print and Design Studio, Stevens Point, Wisconsin

Library of Congress Control Number: 2022949284
ISBN: 979-8-9869663-6-6

This is a work of fiction. Names, characters, businesses, places, events, and incidents are either the products of the author's imagination or used in a fictitious manner. Any resemblance to actual persons, living or dead, or actual events is purely coincidental.

Cornerstone Press titles are produced in courses and internships offered by the Department of English at the University of Wisconsin–Stevens Point.

DIRECTOR & PUBLISHER   EXECUTIVE EDITOR
Dr. Ross K. Tangedal   Jeff Snowbarger

SENIOR EDITORS
Lexie Neeley, Monica Swinick, Kala Buttke

PRESS STAFF
Ellie Atkinson, Grace Dahl, Lauren Engelbreth, Hannah Fenrick, Patrick Fogarty, Angela Green, Cal Henkens, Brett Hill, Julia Kaufman, Catriona Scheinost, Maria Scherer, Taylor Schmidt, Cash Van Stiphout, Matt Vancik, Abbi Wasielewski

For Leah and our sons: Jonny, Joey, Vito, and Nino
And for my mother and father

Also by James B. De Monte:

Brotherhood

Contents

Last Rites

As long as you speak from the lips of the people,
we can be sure that the valley will endure.

—Sergio de Carneri
"In Praise of the Nones Language"

Author's Note

See:

This was all supposed to be about the elevation of the ordinary initially, to put you up on a pedestal. At its most ambitious, it was to turn you into some kind of saint.

And maybe you *will* be dead by the end of this writing, long gone, kicked the bucket, went away with the rest of them. Certainly, what follows will be the best case for your remembrance moving forward, for memoriam, for anyone anywhere giving a damn about a son of foreigners, a disciple of John L. Lewis, a Depression kid who never got over it, the second-oldest living member of the St. Theresa's Knights of Columbus Hall, a pick-and-shovel man.

But let's be clear:

You have not been saintly or even well-mannered or, especially ever, righteous or sanctimonious. Any miracles while alive probably seem unremarkable to most. The one to come? Who knows? You may or may not even believe in God, which would be trouble in the beatification stage. There would be plenty of devil's advocates, too, if the Church still allowed them in this process—none who'd stage significant protest or lose much sleep over it in the end, but plenty who'd wonder why. This part may be worse than not being virtuous: you've never done much of anything or gone anywhere or led any movement.

In truth, most of what follows will be told as if it's happening now and will contain little adventure, little thrill, little more than a *transcribing* of an ordinary life. There are times you'll get close—maybe something big will happen, maybe you'll make an irreversible decision—but we'll settle back in quickly. There will be rabbit dogs and nephews and International two-ton dump trucks and homemade dago red. There will be sadness and ache, joy and acceptance. If there is any divine revelation, that's for you alone, but it sure as hell hasn't happened yet, and it would be hard for anyone else to tell.

Once it starts, it will go fast, especially when it all starts unraveling.

The obstacles to sainthood beyond all this lack of excitement? The only bishops that ever passed through the South Side wouldn't have known you from other Tirolese kids leaving school to dig coal and clay. You've never met a theologian, least of all a cardinal, or a pope, and frequently were beaten by nuns when you were a boy. Before you went to the Catholic school, you'd gone to the country school, and you were beaten by those teachers, too, though they weren't of the cloth. It had nothing to do with your skin or your faith—everyone in this enclave were foreigners and Catholics, too—so even if they'd killed you with a ruler or a switch, martyrdom would have been difficult to argue for. You were just plain acting up and could use a beating.

And now?

Above all else, you've been a brother, and an uncle, and a cousin, and a United Mineworker of America, and briefly a foreman of clay workers making sewer pipe, and a Catholic—*what else would you be?*, and a loyal Democrat—*what else would you be?* You turned 21 in 1944 and voted for all of them ever since. Roosevelt, Truman, Stevenson, Kennedy, Johnson, Humphrey, on and on, Barack Obama, on and on. And a Tyrolean, though you've never left this place. You've been at once Giacomo Agostini and Jack August. Most of all, you remain a true mammone, a devoted son to his mother, thirty years after she's gone. If there's a God and he wanted you to be anything other than any of this, he'd have had you born some place else at some other time to some other people who talked something other than Nones dialect. But you are what you are, and that's the end of it, buddy.

An American? You can vote, and you were born here, like your sister and some of your relations, but an *American?*

There are fewer than twenty stories of you here, some in sequence, some out of it. At the outset, one was to be a reflection of hands, of the hands of everyone around you, of the deep cuts and missing thumbs and soft healing and worn-out, bent-up, crippled claws, but you've never paid much attention to anyone's hands. Why would you? To what end would a story like that even serve? You've never given a firm handshake to anybody anywhere because that's about proving points for the scorekeepers in the generations that have come after you. If there was ever a point to prove, you proved it in the first ninety years of life.

There's a whole lot of death in these stories, not dramatic or thrilling death like on television that you can turn on and off, but just plain old death that sticks with you whether you like it or not. When you're your age, what else do you expect?

Perhaps in the telling of these stories, some case for can-onization *will* become clear, the miracles and so forth, your inclusion in the Litany of Saints, though it likely won't. That is the problem with such endeavors, of dealing with the ordinary. It may just end up being a roughed-out sketch of what's left when the rest of the world has packed up and gone, of what it means to be a blood relative, and of decency.

JBD

Where Are Your People From?

Where Are Your People From?

They meet you in the communal area, past the Welcome Center. Your sister, Helen, is there, along with her son, Willy Jr., and some others. Handful of people. One of Willy Jr.'s boys has a girl with him. It was somebody's birthday and they've brought a pink cake with white frosting, little cherries on top. Polenta with gravy, too. They give you hugs and kisses, ask you how you're feeling, ask you again if you don't answer right away, ask how you've been sleeping, ask if you've been eating anything.

Everybody sits down amongst the artificial plants and upright piano and fireplace with gas logs and filled-up fish tank, and Willy Jr.'s family shows you images of a ship mast and passenger list from Ellis Island. There is a whole pile of papers combined together in a big ringed binder. They are enclosed in plastic sleeves, and the individual sheets of paper are heavy, almost as thick as what they make milk cartons from. These are your mother and father's papers. Helen doesn't say anything, shakes her head at Willy Jr. You know she doesn't have anything to do with it, that she wishes they wouldn't have gone and done this.

The first, Papa's, says LIST OR MANIFEST OF ALIEN PASSENGERS FOR THE UNITED STATES, dated 1914. Arrival: February 15. Passenger ID: 102520190004. This would've been his final trip. Who paid for your passage, they want to know. Are you deformed or crippled? You ever been here before? He'd had, of course, but he didn't check that box. Are you going to see any relatives? Why? Who are they? What are their names? How many vowels? Where do they live? By the river? By the tracks? How many wives do you have? An anarchist? White? *How* white? An Austrian? An Italian? How far south? Any other marks? Do you have a ticket? Do you have fifty dollars? If not, how much do you have? Empty your pockets. Have you been to prison? An almshouse? A nuthouse? Somewhere supported by charity? Were you promised a job here? Is that what you're here for? Can you read, can you write? What's your final destination?

Images of two of the ships Papa came in on are in there. The first is the *Saint Paul*, an American ship. William Cramp & Sons Shipbuilders, Philadelphia, Pennsylvania. Nearly 12,000 tons. Steam quadruple expansion engines. Built for the Navy to fight off the Spanish in 1898. Two funnels, two masts, huge deck, and lots of flags flying on it are really all you can make out on this five-inch by seven-inch photograph. American flags, you can be sure. Number of passengers: 1,370. 350 first class, 220 second class, 800 third class. Does that include the insane? The anarchists? The polygamists? The children that made it or didn't make it? Does that include those who had less than fifty dollars? Who even had fifty dollars in those days? The ship was scrapped in Germany in 1923, according to these papers.

The second ship for Papa in here is called *La Champagne*. Compound engines, single screw. Service speed: 17 knots. Number of passengers: 1,055. 390 first class, 65 second class, 600 third class. Two funnels, four masts. Built for the French. The flags are French. Wrecked somewhere in the South of France in 1915.

Who the hell cares? That's the question everyone ought to be asking.

The passenger list is included with this one. Slovaks, Welsh, Italian Norths—what they're calling your people. Mrs. Tomazoli from Center Street is listed on this one, too. Arrival date: August 9, 1903. That's Willy Jr.'s younger son's birthday, August 9, and the boy lets everybody know it. He's full of pepper.

You close the binder and shut your eyes while they start talking to each other. You recall the story of your cousin, Clementina, the only daughter of Zio Federico and Zia Giusseppina, born in between Moon and Norman. She came over and started elementary school here when Zio Federico returned with his family, the year you were born, but moved to Cleveland as soon as she was a teenager and could type. But back before all of that, when she was small, maybe five or six, and fair-complected and on the boat, Zio couldn't find her. They looked all over and finally got tipped off about the Polack off by himself with the little girl. Or, was it a Croatian?

What's the difference anyway?

Zio Federico held a knife to the Polack's throat and took little Clem back. He should have thrown the Polack overboard but left him, unscathed really. He was man enough to do it, Zio Federico, you know that. Some other Polack tried to explain to your zio that the man had lost a daughter and wife in their country. That's why he was taking children, trying to, and your cousin was fair, like his people. Most of the Polacks, you know, ended up in Cleveland and weren't that fair-skinned, carving marble along with the Sicilians, making steel.

Here's the kicker: Clementina married a Slovak or Polack or Croatian—they're all over the place up there—later in life, thirties probably, no kids, when she was working as a bookkeeper for a union contractor. She never had children, though, and traveled back and forth to your mother and father's hometown. She went on cruises. She hiked in the Alps. She visited the Vatican and was reprimanded for not having her shoulders covered. That's some story, she'd told Helen. They'd telephone each other at one time, and still send cards. She's mid-nineties now, and still has her mind, Helen says, still up in Cleveland.

When you open your eyes, the binder's back open and Willy Jr.'s explaining that they don't have Papa's middle trip included. The only other thing in his section is an image, which, Willy Jr. tells you, they have printed with their own home computer. It's an old crest, blue trim around the whole thing. Across the top is UNITED MINEWORKERS. Underneath that are two hands shaking in the middle, one coming in from the left and one coming in from the right. They are gold. Beneath that is written OF AMERICA. Below that is 8 HOURS. Willy Jr.'s family has made the backdrop an American flag.

Your mother's section is printed on paper with a purple flower border around the edges, looks like lilacs. Mama had come over on a ship called *La Lorraine*, this pile of papers says. They say it was an old World War I armed merchant cruiser. Two funnels, two masts. Steam triple expansion engines. Number of passengers: 1,114. 446 first class, 116 second class, and 552 third class.

You know that's all bullshit, and you tell them all. Mama came on an Irish ship called *The Adriatic*. You'll never forget this, because she told you this much herself once when you were first working at the sewer pipe. There was a red-faced, stout, half-drunk Protestant there from Belfast and you could barely understand him. Mama nearly tripped over herself in the kitchen at home and you told her she was dancing a jig like old Doherty the clay worker, and that got you two talking about Northern Ireland, a new country back then. Mama always felt the Celtic people, so different than yours, were the most attractive people, had the nicest features. In the kitchen, she recalled that ship she came in on and its name, *The Adriatic*. She said they were jammed in like livestock and never mentioned anything about first class or second class or any class. She was alone, 18 years old, motherless and fatherless, at the bottom of the bottom class.

Your sister, Helen, says she thinks that's right. She's pointing at you and becomes more convinced the more she thinks about it. Jackie's right, she tells everybody else, Mama did say that.

Willy Jr.—your nephew, Helen's son, your mother's grandson—taps the binder and says not according to these papers. Your mother, his grandmother, may have had it wrong. She couldn't really read or write very well, he says.

Not in English, you tell him, but she went to school back in Cles.

There her name is, right there, Willy Jr. says. He says he remembers your mother getting mixed up, especially in old age. She wasn't a dumb person, Willy Jr. knows, but she used to get mixed up, don't forget. She'd probably forgotten, he says. Maybe she saw something on television and mixed it all up, his wife says. The problem is, Willy Jr. says, the facts get mixed up with the stories, get lost as time moves on. The important thing to know, they tell you, is that your people came over the right way. That's a fact nobody can dispute, they say.

You tell them what they can do with their facts. This seems to put them off.

Nobody says anything for a while and Helen tells you to eat.

The older boy's girlfriend, sitting next to him with her hands folded over her lap, was runner-up for the Clayweek Festival , Willy Jr. says. She's a big, smiley girl. "Only problem is," Willy Jr. says, "she's a vegetarian. But we're working on her."

She's eating something, that's for sure. At one time, being a beauty queen meant something, you think. Helen could've been Miss Uhrichsville, but she didn't have the personality for it. You two weren't outgoing like your cousins.

Willy's boy and his girlfriend are part of a youth group. They are heading off to Nicaragua to dig latrines for poor people there. "They'll be using a pick and shovel like you, Uncle Jackie," Willy Jr. says.

Like you? "Latrines, huh. What the hell you think you're going to accomplish for those people over there?" you ask.

The girl's been before and starts on about how they can do the work, the people there, but they can't afford supplies, which the American kids will supply. Really, she says, the American kids gain more from the experience than the Nicaraguan people. It's about mutual connection, she says.

"And they are spreading the Word of the Lord," Willy's wife says.

"Oh good," you say. "Otherwise, they'd be shitting in the ground without ever learning about the blood of the lamb." That shuts them up.

After everybody's been quiet for a little bit again, you point over at the girl, "Where are your people from?"

Willy Jr. starts telling her what you mean by that. "I know," she says, "he asked me last time. I'm a little of everything. Heinz 57."

Since Willy's wife and him have gotten more interested in ancestry, they learned she's more Dutch than German, believe it or not, they tell you. They both are taking DNA tests, spitting in little cups, and sending them off so that someone in a lab can tell them what percentage of whatever they are, telling them who they are. They are interested for their children's sake, and you actually get to learn a fair amount of what you might be predisposed to, they say. They'd really like it if you and Helen, Willy's mother, would consider doing the same.

"Oh, Dio," Helen says and puts her hand on her forehead.

This is important information, according to Willy Jr., for disease prevention if nothing else.

They may find out some things they don't want to find out, you think to yourself. There are some things better left dying off with time, who belongs to who and so forth. Who knows what anybody really is, where anybody is really from? And who the hell wants to know what might get them in the end, what disease they're going to get to die from? Who in their right mind? You've never been overly interested in religion, but if this isn't biting from the Tree of Knowledge, somebody should tell you what is.

In between all these papers and the very end of the binder are lots of blank sleeves. Willy Jr. explains that these are for papers you might have left at the house—they have to go through them all yet—old photographs, anything that can be added. This is a living document—evergreen, dynamic—he tells you, something that will remain with the family after you're gone, and after he's gone. Even after his boys are gone. This will go on living, he says. This will go on living.

This plastic pile of nothing will go on living.

The rest of them go on talking awhile, like you're not here, except once in a while Helen gives you a look that's full of something like sadness, or maybe remembrance, and sometimes the young ones look over at you and then quickly away if you look back, as if you're a cripple in a sideshow. You don't know how long it is before you fall asleep and how long it is before you wake back up, binder on your lap.

They start putting their coats on.

"Where the hell's everybody going?" you ask.

"Everybody's got somewhere to go, Jackie," Helen says, tying her scarf, and rubs your back between your shoulders. "I'll be back tomorrow," she says.

"I think they're probably playing football today on the T.V., Cleveland, Pittsburgh, something. Why don't you visit awhile?" you tell everybody.

"Maybe next time we stop in," Willy Jr. says, dressed to leave, "we'll have more of this all sorted out." He takes his binder with him.

The boys and their mother give you kisses on your cheeks and the girl waves goodbye. Some nurse or nun or somebody starts walking towards your chair.

Names of Those Who Have Been
Made Citizens Lately

On Papa's tombstone, it says LOUIS AUGUST. Papa spent close to half a century as Luciano Agostini, and about six days as Louis August, and there it is on his marker, over at the old Catholic cemetery. You can still see it, if the weeds aren't grown up too much. It's flat on the ground, Papa's marker.

Mama buried what was left of him in a brown suit, but by rights, it should've been black as coal dust. He came home so late sometimes, you couldn't even see anyone walking if you looked outside. His face. His hands. Everything all covered. You think you could've seen his teeth if he'd smiled when he walked. His teeth were real white. Not like Zio's, so stained from all that Mail Pouch. Floating teeth. That's what it would've looked like at night. Papa never smiled when he came home from work, though, seven or eight bucks a day in his pocket.

Around the War, and right after, on into Korea, you mowed St. Theresa's for Father Harrington, the old grave-yard and the new one, too. Remember, he used to mow it all himself. Father Harrington was built a lot like Papa, even though he was an Irishman who drank corn whiskey. About five-three or four and a big chest like one of the oak barrels Papa and Zio'd make vin in. No two ways about it, Father Harrington was a tough old bird, but at the end of his rope in the '40s and '50s. So you took over for him. Mama was still living, and you still went to Mass on Sunday. After Mass let out and you'd drive Mama up to the house, you'd mow for Father. When it comes down to it, you spent more time with Papa while mowing at St. Theresa's than you did when he was living.

* * *

Father Harrington didn't say a whole lot when they buried your father and your uncle. He tried saying something in your language, remember, to you and Helen and your cousins about Papa and Zio believing in God and loving Jesus, and other things, too, and that he'd get to sing with the angels. An Irishman trying to speak your language. Somebody should tell you, if God loved them so much, why'd he let that coal fall down on them? Even as a kid, it seemed to you that God's a mean son of a bitch, or he just flat out isn't doing his job. You used to think about that when you'd mow, even when you'd take Holy Eucharist. Boy, Sister would've slapped you good. Said if you thought about anything else other than Jesus Christ during Holy Eucharist, you'd go suffer the eternal flames of Hell. Well, Sister, Father said Papa and Zio thought about Jesus a lot, and there are still parts of them crushed underground in the old Rosemarie mine. You don't know if you'd rather be burned or crushed.

And besides, Papa never went to Mass; that's what Mama did. Zio went regular, too, but Papa never went. You don't ever remember Papa mentioning God or the Holy Mother or Jesus Christ or anything. Never saw him bless himself with holy water. You did once see him tell a young priest in English to go get a job when he asked for money.

10

If there was one thing Papa hated, probably more than anything, it was being called Italian, being called a *dago*. Italiani come from places like Calabria, Napoli, Milano. You did have the same kinds of names, spoke the same kind of language, but you weren't Italians.

You remember when you were a kid, hauling 'shine for Mr. Salvadori. That old bootlegger and countryman of Papa gave you a geography lesson of sorts. Mr. Salvadori spoke good English, especially to your people, the young ones anyway. He was looking at a map spread out across his supper table. It was a colored map, and Austria was yellow on it. South Tyrol, the northeast of today's Italy, was inside the yellow. You stood beside him and didn't say a whole lot. He showed you where your people came from. Trento was inside the yellow, sure, but it was on the border.

Papa had left Italy or Tyrol or Austria or whatever you want to call it, depending when you showed up to Ellis Island and what you wrote down. Left it three times. Zio Federico went back after the last time, started his family, and then brought them all back here a decade later.

You asked Mr. Salvadori about the Siciliani from Grant Street. He took a straight edge he had sitting at the table and drew a line from French Tunisia and the rest of North Africa on through Sicily. He showed you a good part of Sicily sits farther south than North Africa. He said that ought to give you an idea of what the Siciliani are.

You asked him, "Then what are we?"

"Tyroleans," he said in English, which you knew, of course, of course. He told you it was Mussolini who made your people Italians, justified by Roman tablets they found in Cles, your father's hometown, Mr. Salvadori's hometown. The people in Val di Non had requested Roman citizenship before Christ, and by God if they weren't Italian to this day, according to Mussolini.

Mr. Salvadori showed you the old papers, too, the old copies of the *Daily Times*, years before it ever got bought out by the *Recorder*. He showed you editions from 1904 when he'd come over that introduced everybody to the "quaint Tyroleans." The paper said the Tyrolean wasn't the brightest man, but he was a real man—whatever that means. The paper compared your people to mountain goats, said you wear goat tails on your hats and stockings on your legs. It said your people are hard to shake but always up for a scrap. It said you are brave peasants with honest hearts and homely faces. It said your people have features no other peasant race in Europe shares: small feet and neat ankles. It said when all else fails, you yodel, a floor-thumping, thigh-slapping call; spirited, but modest, full up of mountain air. Yodel. That's what this paper said.

Another piece he'd had from the same year, on the *front* page, said, NAMES OF THOSE WHO HAVE BEEN MADE CITIZENS LATELY. It had Matteries, Zanolinis, Gasperettis, Menapaces, Tomazolis, Zanons, Polletes, Bergamos, Endrasses, Fondriests, Visintainers, DeBiasis, Chinis. Everybody. Welsh, Germans, even Norwegians, too. Sicilians, Calabrians. Mr. Salvadori. Papa. Everybody. The paper said all of your people declared themselves willing to "fight, bleed, and die for free America." Why wouldn't they declare that?

The article underneath, you'll never forget: THE TIME IT TAKES TO COUNT A MILLION ONE-DOLLAR BILLS.

These were different times, remember.

*　*　*

Mr. Salvadori was a hook-nosed, Tyrolean bootlegger who, you came to find out later, beat up on his red-headed wife,

Flora, who was a distant cousin to Mama, and whose maiden name was already Salvadori to begin with. His best customer, Mr. Mazzarrone, a hooked-nosed Sicilian if you ever saw one, lived on Grant Street, was a cop, wouldn't call himself Italian either, and did the same thing to his wife. Though, Helen says both those wives, Mr. Salvadori's and Mr. Mazzarrone's, were quite the actresses, really.

Only black person you really knew at the time was Chicken Thompson, who sold slabs of ice out of a flatbed truck. He's about the blackest man you ever saw in your whole life, and like the rest of them, lived over near Jackson's Sewer Pipe. You never said much to him, but the blacks at the Golden Rod mine knew him. Probably a relation. Told you, old Chicken Thompson never hurt a fly. But who knows: maybe he beat up his wife, too.

Anybody asks you, you were all in the same boat, a sinking ship shot full of holes by Uncle Sam and Herbert Hoover and Benito Mussolini and Ettore Tolomei and Pope Pius and everybody else sitting at the top.

* * *

When Papa finally settled down here, there were probably three or four-thousand people on the South Side alone. On top of that, just about everybody was a coal miner, or else they found work in the rail yard. You could be waving a red, white, and green Italian flag or a white and red Tirolese flag or whatever-colored flag you got in your left hand and in your right was a red, white, and blue Lady Liberty-approved pickaxe.

At that point, Mama lived in Europe still and looked after the little ones that belonged to the Baron of Cles. You've not been to Europe, and, of course, you don't ever expect to go, but you saw a sketch once of the castle Mama worked in. A more recent portrait. In it, the castle sat on a hill, looking over most of Cles, the biggest town in all of Val di Non. You can still see it in your head, lots of little homes spread out over the hillside, tucked into mountains. The top of the castle was a kind of red, and it had Tirolese flags hanging off, flipped sideways, which look like Austrian flags with red bars and the eagle in the middle.

Mama said they used to cultivate silk and hemp there in Cles, but never really talked about Val di Non too much. She showed pictures and smiled when she did. She tried to learn English and did all right for a while, she said. Problem was, your people started moving to the South Side in droves, some Mama's age, some she grew up with in Cles. Once that all started, Mama slipped right back to your language, isolated, effetto montagna. According to your cousin Calimero, who sends Christmas cards to all the American relatives, Cles now has about one-thousand Muslims out of six-thousand total. Why not, that's where the work is. He bellyaches about it, just like an American would've complained about Papa and Mama being a couple of Wops.

Mama must've had Carmela right after she arrived, but she and Papa said Carmi was born later. It's hard to say. Carmi was baptized here at St. Theresa's, you do know that, but died from influenza when you were very small, too young to ever remember. You never knew her, but you did know Ines. She was the Salvadoris' last daughter who died when the house burned up. Suffocated from the smoke. That fire was terrific, made the sky orange, orange as Mrs. Salvadori's hair. You never saw a fire like that one. Little Ines wasn't many months more than a year when she died. At the funeral Mass, Mama stood with one arm around Helen, who was so young herself, both of them holding onto rosaries. You can still see Mrs. Salvadori up front, a cold ghost, not even weeping, her bright hair sticking to her white face.

It was the old man's still that caused that fire, and he went back to making 'shine before too long. You remember thinking about your dead older sister, Carmi, and figured that was about as close to knowing her as you'd ever get. And you remember it was only two or three days after Mr. Salvadori showed you his map.

* * *

The day your name changed—officially, on papers—you'd come home and were fixing to go down along the tracks with Coke Haas to find some coal. You and Coke used to get good coal when you were nine, ten, eleven years old. Come down right off the car. And sometimes, when the trains were stopped, you and Coke would shimmy up the side and take a little off the top. Long as you can remember, you never had to buy coal during the cold months, not once.

A freight train had gone by that particular morning, according to Mama. Before you left, Mama stopped you, almost like she had some kind of secret that only you were supposed to know, and pointed at some papers sitting on the table. One said JACK AUGUST. You didn't say anything either way and just went out.

Coke, a big pale kid with a flat nose, asked you on the way, "Hell was that about, Jack?"

"Hell if I know," you told him and kept going.

While you and Coke were gathering coal, he started on about the foreigners taking the working man's jobs. Said his mother hadn't been able to fix a whole lot for supper and his old man told him it was on account of the Wops and Polacks coming in and making it rough for the working man to get by. Normally, you'd have popped anybody right in the mouth for saying that kind of shit. Mainly because your mother and father had their papers, came through Ellis Island, and weren't drunk or crazy like Polacks. Probably knocked a couple of teeth out, too. But Coke and you were close, so instead you told him, "Reason you Krauts don't have no food is on account of your old man being a little too thirsty all the goddamn time." Papa told you that, and it was true. You'd hauled 'shine to Coke's old man's place over that past year several times.

Anyway, you should've popped Coke, but he got you first instead. You didn't even bleed. And right after is when you came across some old zinginer sitting up on a rusted-up railroad car. You'll never forget, one of his feet went the opposite way. That zinginer told you, "Come on over here boys. I got something to show you." The bastard wasn't wearing any pants and you saw Coke take off running the other way. You did, too.

Most of the zingari lived in tents down in the Bottoms, across Route 250, setting up camp every year. This one must have wandered off. Really, the Americans had some nerve blaming any of your people.

*　*　*

Wasn't long after Papa got killed in the Rosemarie mine that you got the hell out of St. Theresa's and started digging coal for the Reynolds Brothers. Your first job in the mines was running the ponies down in the shaft to take loads here to there. And you don't care what anyone tells you, down there it doesn't matter where your people are from, how greasy or nappy your hair is, which direction your hooked nose leans, nothing. By the end of the day, your face is black, blacker than Louis Armstrong's. Blacker than Chicken Thompson's.

Your arms, your legs, everything is black, even underneath your clothes. It doesn't make one lick of difference. You're all the same below ground. You ended up working with Coke Haas, Cousin Norman, Willy Horvath, and a bunch of other St. Theresa's boys; every one of you black as hell by quitting time, looking like a goddamn minstrel show. It's a miracle any of you are living today.

Somebody ought to go find that 1904 newspaper with the New Americans, all of those quaint Tyroleans who love to fight and look like homely goats. Then somebody ought to go get the full list of the Rosemarie dead and see how many of those New Americans finally got their chance to fight, bleed, and die for free America.

Effetto Montagna

Deep down, three and a half miles from the mine mouth, is where they blew Papa up and buried what parts they never would recover of him. This was in January, icicles looming like raised pickaxes.

Most of the other dead came from nearby, too, everybody in little camps with their own people, all talking their own language.

Somebody said it was powder smoke. Somebody said it was the very dust of the coal. Somebody else said it was oil dripping from the roof. Cousin Norman knew it was white damp.

The president of the Ohio District of the United Mineworkers told you all that you'd get compensation, your fathers' burials paid for by the state, or the company, or somebody.

Temporary morgues were put up in pool halls and beer joints. The Blue Goose is where your zio, Federico, lay, overcooked and grimy. New widows and orphans and old priests and young nuns and curious spectators and dazed miners blocked the roadways. Mrs. Leotta from Grant Street lost all three sons: Beppo, Lino, and Popeye.

Rescue workers went in without masks, fought through tunnels half-collapsed and strewn with timber and steel beams. Other miners, whose eardrums had been cracked in half, blocked air with makeshift brattices of burlap and wood. The Slovak fire boss who Papa never trusted to begin with found most of him about an hour after they got the others. *The Daily Recorder* celebrated the Slovak fire boss for his bravery, for risking himself to find the dead. His people had come here at the same time as yours and lived in Barn-hill, and he used to go to Mass before he divorced his wife.

Of course, there were a lot who made it out, plenty more than who got blown up. But nobody beats a coal mine: white damp got Papa straight away, and black damp probably got the Slovak fire boss somewhere down the line.

* * *

And don't forget:

The State Industrial Commission has heeded the lessons of the terrible accidents in Pennsylvania and West Virginia. And the State Industrial Commission has worked diligently to promote mine safety education. And the State Industrial Commission has forbidden taking blasting powder in or out of haul-ways with electric wires, the blasting powder you miners have bought yourselves. And the State Industrial Commission will work exhaustively to determine the exact cause of *this* explosion. And the State Industrial Commission will be sure the limestone solution is sprayed adequately, to subdue the dust. And the State Industrial Commission will pay your family eighteen dollars and seventy-five cents a week for the next seven years. And the State Industrial Commission will pay your family one-hundred and fifty dollars *right now* for the burial.

And the Rosemarie mine will be reopened by February. The bituminous door of the big coffin opened back up.

* * *

Are you not eating? Are you not sleeping in homes with roofs over your heads? Are your children not in schools, receiving a Catholic or a public education? Are libraries not being built? Are the pews not full on Sunday? Are you not free to sit in those pews? Are the roads not now being paved?

This is the cost of industrializing. This is the cost of mass production. This is the cost of private individuals having the right to breathe freely and earn a living. This is the cost of lessons learned. This is the cost of manifest destiny. This is the cost of assimilation.

This is *the* cost of one slim crust of bread.

This is *the* cost of effetto montagna.

This is the cost of us letting you people in here to begin with.

The Poor, the Crippled,
the Lame, the Blind

You were the darkest in the whole gang. Your cousins used to say you belonged to the peddler, the one with the long, dented up Gray Motor Company Coach. A Syrian was something hard to understand, his way of speaking making him sound distinguished, elevated, above you all, but sometimes like he was about to cough something up. He'd only come through the South Side once in a great while when you were old enough to remember, not like he did when you were real small, Mama said.

"Mizzez Agostini, Mizzezz Agostini!" the peddler would call before he was even fully out of his automobile. He seemed like he was always in motion, spreading all his inventory for display. Mama would hold a hand in her apron and move her fingers over colorful wares spread out on a wool blanket, like she was playing a gospel hymn at Mass. These were brand new, but, while it was hard to put your finger on it, there was something, even in those days, that you knew was slightly askew compared to other new things you'd seen other places.

"Oh! Mizzezz Agostini, for you, for you," and the price would come down, explained some place where Syrian and English and your dialect met, maybe the only place they met, here on the South Side, here on top of the coal and the clay, walking distance from the mine mouth. Mama would shake her head no, no, of course not. Too much. She'd wave him off. "Wait, Mizzezz Agostini, wait!" There was always more for that price. Of course it wasn't just the dish. A copper pan. A wooden doll. Silken Chinese scarves. A tin cup. A small drawing of a Russian tsar on a deck of playing cards. A baseball even!

The Syrian peddler would then sit with Mama, and they'd have coffee, which she made like it was Sunday, like Zio and Zia and everybody else who spoke what you spoke were all coming by to visit awhile. You would sit with your sister and your big cousins, Moon and Clementina and Norman, and listen in. His hair was slicked back, gray at the temples. His mustache bent down on each side towards the bottom of his cheeks. His eyes bent down the same direction. The skin under his chin hung towards his shirt collar. Told you he was a type of Catholic, different than your people, but a sort of Catholic just the same. His wife back there, over there, in the old place, was nowhere to be found one morning. He couldn't stay there.

A banshee!, the old wife.

Mama laughed that laugh when her cheeks would get big for effect, like she was holding in all the air for a minute, honoring all that intended orneriness in the Syrian's dead-pan telling, and she'd blow it out, shaking in her shoulders with laughter. Your mother, this woman who wouldn't dare speak English if she went into town, could make sense of all this broken, tangled nonsense from the Syrian peddler. His current wife here was not much better than the old one, sure. He'd kept up with peddling to be left alone for a while, to get her off his back. He'd hobble around for us like some great weight was clinging on him. She was a fat woman, he said. Mama would wave him off. He expanded his arms for all of you, the children. She was fat, believe him. You never saw fat people, really. Sure, maybe one or two, but seldom ever. Could that wife of his be as fat as he claimed? Could a person be so fat?

You remember how the peddler told you he'd spent two weeks making tube for Timken Steel in Canton, a good living, where he lived with his American family. Two weeks. Enough. You remember the time he'd told you all how he could tell his own fortune, each morning. That particular morning, for example, he knew he would have a wonderful day, that the sun would shine just brightly enough and his automobile would operate perfectly without trouble, and his wife would not be angry at the trivialities of the world, and your own mother would find prized treasures amongst his collection. He would tell you this all mostly with his hands. Why? How could he know all this before the day even began? He was no god, no churchman, no zinginer with a crystal ball. Why? Because he'd gone to his chicken coop that morning and found just one egg, only one, but when he'd brought it back in to prepare for himself, it was a double yolk. Two deeply golden orbs, each like the sun above, one slightly bigger than the other, like him and his dead twin brother, he said. A day that would begin with a double yolk, the Syrian peddler told you, was impossible to be a bad day—unless, of course, it was. He would pat you all on the head before he'd leave, nearly always. You liked when the peddler came usually, but didn't like being told that you belonged to him by your cousins because your skin darkened in the sun as his did.

*　*　*

There's lots you've forgotten, but you won't forget this: the last time you ever saw the peddler, he'd brought with him a small boy, probably two or so, who crawled from the back of the Gray motor car. His hair was blond—not at all like the peddler's coal black with a little gray—though dusty with dirt, and did not appear to have been cut, ever at all.

Who did he belong to?

The little boy had on the old kind of cloth that stuck out of his short pants, and no shoes. You all had shoes. Poor as you were, hungry as anyone else on the South Side, you all had shoes. Another man was with the peddler, too, equally as dusty as the child, old enough to be the boy's grandfather. At some point, the older man did step away towards some place or other, lighting a little cigar as the Syrian was unloading, mumbling about frustrations with his company for the day, and the boy of not much more than two ran up to you all, rambling in his language, up to your dog, Peaches, back to the Gray motor car, over to where you'd kept the hog, and around and around. The peddler was keeping an eye on him while the other man kept walking, smoking. Your sister, Helen, was laughing sweetly, witness to the whole scene like you, but Mama seemed upset and didn't buy anything from the Syrian peddler that last time. You will always feel a bit empty when you think of that little boy, of how hard the world might have ended up for him.

* * *

Others came to see Mama, too, all sorts who were down-trodden, out of luck, crippled up, couldn't see, couldn't hear, and looking for mercy. There was a bum who showed up, maybe four times a year, once a season. He looked awful. Small curls of hair on his forehead, never shaven, a sunken-in belly that made his clothes too big for him, clothes made for someone else to begin with, no doubt. An old woolen coat, at least, year-round, and cardboard in his shoes. Everyone was hungry in those days, sure, but some were hungrier, some left behind even in those times when it seemed everyone had been left behind. He was a traveler, maybe part zinginer, with an accent you couldn't quite make out, but his English was as good as yours. "God bless you, ma'am, God bless you."

Papa told Mama not to bother, that Jesus Christ himself said you'd always have bums, but she couldn't help it. "He smiles big and sad like my brother," she would say in your people's language. "He limps when he moves up the steps like Zio Damiano," she would swear. "His heart has been broken by a hard world." Mama would let him into the kitchen. She would make him coffee with lots of cream. She had sandwiches for him when he'd come. He seemed as grateful to her for all this good will as anyone anywhere could be.

These were different times, remember.

Only once did he come when Papa was home, a Sunday, and Papa—for all his griping, for all his swearing off of the bum—was just as decent to him as Mama. Maybe he knew he would be; maybe that's why he didn't want him around in the first place. Papa and the bum sat and talked for a long while. How did they make any sense to each other, in their own languages, you wondered. They must've known just enough. And they used their hands, they debated, they laughed. They played morra. *Morra!* Mama served them both, Papa and the bum. She fixed them plates of polenta and gravy, gave them each slices of chocolate cake with caramel topping, the American kind she learned about when they'd visited relations in Hopedale, closer to the river, amongst Americans and everybody else; the kind she seldom made, but when she did, it was a Sunday. They drank table wine. They had coffee. She patted Papa finally, though. "Luco, Luco." Snapped him out of his trance. Papa stood up and smiled. The bum took his cue.

He would turn up again, but not on Sundays, and Mama would fix coffee with lots of cream and a sack full of sand-wiches. He stopped after a while, sometime down the line, after Papa was gone and you were older. You can remember Mama wondering where he'd gone, what had happened to him. He was like her brother, she'd said, like her uncle, his heart broken in half by the hardness of the world.

Blood Relations

Old-World Chit-Chat

In Helen's kitchen, thick noodles lie strewn across the counter-top, drying. Though it's small overall, there is a fireplace right in the kitchen, too. Helen and Willy Sr. had a fireplace in just about every room in the house, this one with white and black brick built up around it. Above it, a mantel. On that are pictures of her grandsons, a double frame with her son's senior portrait on one side and his wedding photograph on the other, one of her dead husband, and still, even today, a photograph of John L. Lewis, miners' patron saint, bushy-eyed and big-jawed. A clock is in the middle and a crucifix hangs, fixed into the mortar of the brick behind it, dried palms from some Passion Sunday past tight behind the cross.

You've brought over chrysanthemums for her, and sit down at the top of the steps to start unlacing your boots. "Pretty sloppy out there today, Lena."

"Oh, Jesus, Jackie. Keep them on. Look at this place. You think I want you to take your shoes off. I'm embarrassed to even have company. Look at this place." She places the flowers on her supper table. "Get up," she says. "Get up."

There isn't dust anywhere in this house. There isn't a cobweb in a corner. There is plastic on the davenport in the front room. There are strawberries on the wall, yellow paper. They'd hung it in the late 1970s, must have been, and that yellow has faded, yes, but there has never been dirt in your little sister's kitchen. You leave your laces undone, boots still on, and sit at the table.

"Willy came over here today with my ballot." Her voice trembles when she talks, these last couple years, everything a little shaky. She's thinner than Mama, and her hair is always fixed, but anymore she looks like the past.

"Oh dandy, another one again, huh? When are they going to give up on having these? When have they done anyone any good?" you ask.

"Little Angelo had to tell me who the Democrats are after ten o'clock Mass. You know he's eighty-eight now?" She laughs. "Anyway, they don't tell you what party the judges are. Who knows what difference it makes?" Her hands move side-to-side a bit as she unfolds a scrap of paper on which she has inscribed candidates' names. "Oh Madonna, I can't read or write anymore." She shoves it over to you, pushing a small metal pin out of the way she'd used for punching the ballot. "Take it if you want it, Jackie. Just don't tell Willy who's on it."

"One side gives you a little bit," you say and rub your thumb on the first two fingers of your left hand. "And the other side, nothing at all. Pretty straightforward, pretty simple to figure out. If you're going to vote, ain't hard to figure out who for."

"Heavens, yes, Jackie, but that's not how people feel anymore. You should see the signs people have up out Route 800. Homes that can't even keep their lights on, keep their water running, some of them our people. You should see the signs they put up. If they had money, sure."

"That's another story," you agree.

"But people with nothing," she says. "Can you imagine? Imagine if Papa were alive today, what he'd have to say about it."

"He'd give all those people a kick in the ass," you say.

Helen blows out some laughter and says, "Anyway." She mumbles something in your language and then starts telling you about how Pat Sajak was teasing one of the contestants the night before —"He's bad," she says—and then how another one, during the introductions, hadn't really had any children but told Pat she did and started talking about her Dalmatians, about how they were her children. "Imagine!" Helen says. This woman, according to Helen, goes on, during the introductions, about all of her ailments. She's a young woman, remember, Helen tells you, and lists everything wrong with her—accidents, bone disease, the whole lot. "She says all that on television, to everybody," Helen says. "People were private at one time. Women knew better, Jackie. Mama would've rather died than let anyone—let alone a T.V. audience!—know about those sorts of things."

You laugh and say that's right.

"Why," Helen says, "no wonder that woman doesn't have a husband, and good luck convincing one now."

She starts on to something about All Souls' Day Mass times, something about not having to go since it's not really a Holy Day of Obligation. She's saying how she was thinking about that in the middle of the night, since that's when she does all her worrying, feeling like she's drowning in a glass of water, but then it must hit her all at once. "Giacomo, carnederli!" When she talks in your language, her voice smooths out, gets sing-songy again. She gets up and wipes her hands on her apron and gets the bread dumplings from her refrigerator. She has a look on her face like *you* should have been the one to remind *her*. She doles them out with a big plastic spoon, in two bowls, one for each of you, and then goes to heat yours up. You wait and listen to the chiming of the clock, curved oak, the way old clocks used to all look placed atop mantels.

Your baby sister is shuffling around now, fumbling with who-knows-what, when the microwave finally dings. "Tell me if it's not hot enough. I can put it in longer," she says, putting your bowl down in front of you. The syllables stressed and hard each, you know that you and your sister are part of something dwindling away, the remaining bits each breaking up and floating off like a dandelion going to seed.

You start scooping. "Fine, just fine." You prefer room temperature, to get all the flavor.

"Buona forchetta," she says, grabbing your shoulder, and sits down. She starts explaining to you, the way people used to tell stories, the way all the details in a spoken story mattered at one time, that she used salami, the old-fashioned hard kind, used chunks of it, and bacon, broth, onion, parsley, and the rest. She tells you this in your people's language. Then she says, "What about a sandwich, too? I have Genoa salami for that. Melts in your mouth, Jackie. And provolone."

"No, no, just the bread gnocchi."

"Tell me if it's not hot enough, Jackie."

You slurp it up fast, the dumplings already gone and the bowl tilted up to your chin, dripping off the afternoon's whiskers. "Hell, these taste like Mama's, Lena. Jesus Christ."

She gets back up and takes your ball cap off as she moves behind you, placing it on a hall tree at the top of the steps. You've still got a pencil behind your ear from earlier in the day. She puts a cloth napkin next to your bowl, sits back down, and never does get to her bowl. Her telephone rings.

"Go ahead," you tell her.

"Oh, somebody trying to sell you something, to be sure," she says.

You get up and pick it up, the cord hanging down to your feet. You can barely make out anything the woman is saying and smile at your sister and say, "Who? No, hell no. I just watch the place for her."

"Stop it, Jackie. Oh, Dio," she says.

"Me?" you ask the person on the other end, still not figuring out what they're really after. "Democrat, we vote Democrat."

"More politics," Helen says.

"Listen lady," you say, "I'd vote for the devil if he were Democrat."

Helen comes and takes the phone from your hand and hangs it back up.

You take your place again at the table. "You ought to tell your boy," you say, wiping your chin with the napkin, "after he stops cashing those compensation checks, after he cancels his union pension, after that wife of his gives back her unemployment"—

"After they stop getting relief dinners for the boys at school," Helen breaks in, her eyes big, looking down at the table, but stops and goes to the breadbox at the countertop, having thought of something else.

"That's right," you say. "Then, tell them to go ahead and vote Republican." It's then that you use an expletive you'd only have used years back in the mine, never in front of your sister, or your mother, or anyone else above ground. What's gotten into you?

Helen ignores—for your sake, it seems. "They get brainwashed, Jackie, you know that, the way people always have. Nothing ever changes. You know that. Café?" she asks, but she's telling more than asking.

It's made, a big percolator going on the stovetop, so you take it. She pours milk and sugar in without asking, places some store-bought pizzelles in front of you, anise flavor, and sits back down. You start dunking.

"Easy, pasticcione!" She takes a dishrag slung over her shoulder and starts wiping up the mess you're making with one hand, her other on your own shoulder. She then starts wiping the crumbs into her hand at the edge of the table, but begins squinting at your coffee cup. "Oh my God," she says, "it's a wonder I can remember anything. I really am an old nonna anymore." She goes to the cabinet and gets you a saucer and a spoon. "There's more pizzelles," she says. "I have Neapolitan ice cream too, if you want a dish. Chocolate syrup. Nobody else is eating it, Jackie."

You start talking more, your mouth full up with coffee-soaked crumbs. "Put 'em all through another Depression," you holler. "See 'em talk that bootstrap bullshit then."

Helen has already started sweeping the linoleum underneath your feet. "The Wheel's coming on," she says, "if you can stick around."

Compensation

The sun's barely up and you step over cracked slate shingles spread out by the stoop. You walk to several windows, trying to peer inside. The siding is the kind of hard gray that sets in after a white farmhouse rots for years, untouched, and the paint chips and chips until nothing is left but bare wood, blackened, full of decay.

The front door has two deadbolts and a chain across it with a heavy lock. You look down at your beagle and say, "Take one hell of a hacksaw, buddy." You walk around the side to look through a dining room window. It's a bit elevated, but you grab the sill. You pull yourself up to see inside. The piano's upstairs, on an open overhang, lofted. You first saw it the past summer when gathering brass washtubs, so Helen could plant petunias in them come spring. As your hands clench, your coat sleeves pull back, your bare forearms pulsing, bulging, nearly popping old buttons. You haven't mined coal or clay for four decades, but, really, you could still if you wanted.

It's an upright piano, looking unblemished except for dust. A bit of light is shooting in from the window, hitting the brass pedals. They shine like buried treasure might, just discovered in some old picture show, the kind they showed over in Uhrichsville at the new theatre. The top edges have brass on them, too, with some inscription on the left, unreadable from here. You suck air between your teeth to concentrate.

Surely, it's of some company of some old American town, proud and boastful and alive once. You can hear Mama playing. Spoke no English, but played the organ at Mass when you were small, every Sunday and Holy Days. Now, the only young ones left are Willy Jr.'s boys, Helen's grandsons, and their mother has them at some holy roller, born-again church. Only guitars, they tell you, no pipe organs.

You clench the sill harder. It won't be long until the roof comes down and smashes the whole goddamn thing. You let go and let yourself fall the foot or so.

You tell Speedy, "Let's get out of here."

* * *

Blood has been splattered between the rhubarb along the narrow creek that you cut for Helen, so that she can make those good pies, and the barbed wire you strung along the property line. It's fresh and stretches away from the path, veering and bending towards the bog down below. Something's dying down there, under gray November sky, and Speedy wants after it.

The beagle's sturdy frame and long ears cause a whole lot of people to ask if he's part basset. You always tell them, "Can't say for sure. I do know that he's a regular, first-class son of a bitch." It's damned good, but the first you never used much for hunting, for much of anything. Truthfully, you probably haven't shot a thing besides rabbit in the last ten years. You haven't gigged frogs for twice that long and have found no use in 'coon pelts since they dropped below twenty dollars apiece. Poor old Speedy, it's all a bit unjust to him.

You go along the barbed wire and off the path, following the blood wherever it goes, walking through briars and poison ivy, which no longer ravages your body—must've become immune all these years in. Your boots shuffle more than stomp these days. Only the birch trees have any leaves left now, lingering ghosts of late autumn rattling in breeze. Now you can see it up ahead: a big buck, probably ten-point and lifeless.

You never hunted them. When you were a kid, you'd never seen deer in Ohio, and by the time they populated and then became over-populated, you'd finished most of your hunting. Hit one once with your International dump, killed it instantly. All in all, though, deer are reserved for today's hunters: sportsmen, guys who hang severed heads on their walls and leave the meat. In your life, you've eaten squirrel, groundhog, possum, snapping turtle, and just about any kind of fish that rises up to the surface after coal-blasting dynamite detonates. Not one of them hangs on your wall, though you have placed a squirrel's tail on your truck's antenna once or twice.

You go over to the buck and bend down, asking Speedy, "Why would any working person take off a day's work to hunt deer?" It's true: everyone has refrigerators now, and packs of bologna only go for a couple of bucks. These are different times. You put your hand on its belly, almost feels warm. Something peaceful about anything freshly dead. It's bow season, but the arrow has been removed, nothing but a bloody hole sucking through damp air.

Now, you've known good men who bow hunt. Truly, there are a whole hell of a lot of them. But there's also a whole hell of a lot of kids-who-never-grew-up using bows and arrows, crossbows even—playing Indians, hunting for trophies. Grown boys who never lived through a Depression, more to the point.

Speedy sniffs about the buck's body, circling around it, and you see that it's only eight-point. "He was an old bugger, wasn't he?" You palm its chest and shift it side to side. "Probably nine, ten years old." You feel the cracks and holes in its antlers, and some furless patches on its face. "He was a fighter. Poor old devil." You hold the antlers in one hand while lifting the head from the ground, and stare into the buck's eyes; their blackness, dense, reflects back the blue of your own, common to your people, Tirolese people. It will lie and rot here, this old deer, dust to dust, a dime a dozen.

You stand up and whistle, and start back towards the house. You walk for a while and figure that your great-nephews, Willy Jr.'s boys, ought to see the piano. Just to get up close, maybe even touch it. Perhaps then those boys would hear their great-grandmother playing, a language not English, not Tirolese, just music playing. Maybe then they won't end up chasing worn-out deer around forests with bows and arrows.

You come to the house and take Speedy to the red plywood box you built for some other dog, which sits between tall pines you'd planted fifty years before. Your now-mostly-white dog circles you a couple or three times and licks your palms, still calloused but the skin thinning out.

A blacksnake goes quick from underneath the box, its bottom half-rotted. You pull the .45 from your hip pocket, point it at the blacksnake, probably four-foot long, and watch it move with the barrel's shadow. You swing your arm horizontally, this way and that, and the snake stays right along with it. You switch the gun to your left hand and keep the snake in place. Now you grab its tail quick and fling the bastard into the creek below. You give Speedy, unbound, one last pet on the head, needing to clean up, because at ten o'clock, Cousin Norman is going to be buried.

At St. Theresa's, there are only about thirty people inside. In fact, probably ten at least are the same old-timers who show up to every funeral, whether they know the guy who kicked the bucket or not, most of them on the verge, too. You drop something in the poor box near the doors and sit next to Helen, the rest of your family in a pew in front of her.

Your nephew has married a genuine witch, probably ten years younger. But, really, that's all the more Willy Jr. deserves, not half the man his late father was, him now off work several months. He is short and squat, awfully stocky like his dad, but not sturdy. His glasses are always cocked on his face, his knit collared shirts stained and un-tucked. A comb-over atop his head makes the mess of Willy Jr. complete.

You can't keep the boys' names straight, but figure at least one is named Willy, too, like their dad, like their long-dead Polack grandpa. You call them Willy both and lean up to them, saying, "You boys know his name ain't Norman, don't you? It's Natale, *Christmas* in other words, in our language. That's the name he come here with, we're the ones that give him *Norman*."

The boys smile at each other.

You lean back. The organ plays and you think boys nowadays really ought to learn an instrument. They don't have to drive pit ponies in coal mines, or keep the doors in the shafts open for ventilation, or haul moonshine for immigrant bootleggers. They can work with their minds, not their backs. They can play an instrument instead of hoisting a pickaxe. A piano is as good as any, and its heavy, solid presence can change their house for the better. And you aren't about to wait for Willy Jr. to think a piano necessary. "Hey," you say, "you boys come up to the house when you get a chance. I got something to show you."

The music continues, and it's not worth thinking about your dead cousin. Norman survived death twice before: when he was hit by a bread truck as a little boy—knocked him half-funny for life—and then again when Cousin Moon got him in an accident by the old cemetery. Besides, there's always somebody dying anymore. You sit back and take inventory of all the paintings and statues your donations to the parish have bought. The altar is different from when you were a kid, the whole thing carpeted, not marble. Jesus hangs dead and mounted on the wall in front of you, and Saint Lucia still holds her eyeballs on a plate next to the confessional. Eventually, some young priest will be bound to decide the new generation at St. Theresa's doesn't need eyeballs on plates to keep them on the straight and narrow and will take her down. Today, she still stands, bloody and mournful.

The new Stations of the Cross look like cartoons now. In the one just to your left, Christ is getting whipped by Roman soldiers, blood dripping from his crown of thorns. You grab the back of the pew in front of you and lean up, saying "Goddamn," louder than you meant to, and your foot hits the kneeler. Your nephews snicker in front, and the witch lady with them scowls. "Best she's ever looked," you mutter. Your baby sister pats your leg.

Now that Norman's dead, Clementina's the last of Zio Federico and Zia Giuseppina's three children. Cousin Moon, Norman's big brother half his size, must've died ten years ago now.

"Where's Clem?" you ask your sister.

"She didn't make it down, Jackie."

"Who the hell's that then?" you ask.

"That's Mildred," your sister says.

"Why's Mildred here?"

"Still married. Norman never divorced her."

Norman had saved, lived like a pauper, and there sat his apparent widow, still and upright, looking like an ice sculpture or something.

"Well, Mildred knew what she was doing," you say. Then you lean up to Willy Jr. and say, "Somebody left an eight-pointer near my property line."

"Probably too old. Bad meat, stringy," Willy Jr. says out the side of his mouth, back at you, staring on at the altar still.

Mass begins and you shut your eyes for part of it. Father Ralph Nowak, red-nosed and well-fed, gives a homily about long lives well lived—he must've never met Norman—and soon enough there is a hymn promising, "He will raise you up, on eagles' wings."

On your way out, they give you a small flag to attach to the top of your vehicle for the procession out to the gravesite, a slow rolling pace. After you park, someone from the funeral home asks if you'd like to serve as a pallbearer now even though you weren't one at the church, so you oblige and help unload Norman from the hearse. You're the seventh man and know there's no real use for you here. Your good shoes shuffle through dewy grass and they sit you up near the casket—"Here, Mr. August, sit here. Mr. August, please, rest your legs."—and you get to listen as the rifles shoot, the trumpet plays, and the priest shines perpetual light upon your cousin.

* * *

At the wake, only twenty or so people sit around, eating creamed chicken sandwiches and sloppy joes, drinking coffee. It's at the school cafeteria, next to the church. Used to be a high school, at one time, before they dozed the old elementary. Everybody after your generation ended up going on to high school. You look over some old pictures scattered out over a round table. There's one of him with Clementina and Moon and one with you and your sister. There is a square box with Norman's service medals pinned in, too. You stay ten minutes and never sit down. Before you leave, though, you remind the boys to stop at the house. "Okay, Uncle Jackie," they say. As you go for the door, Willy Jr. tugs your sleeve and says—if it wouldn't be too much trouble—he needs some number six coal again this year. December's nearing, and things are getting cold as hell.

You say, "All right," and leave.

*　*　*

When you get home, you change from your jacket and tie and put on a flannel shirt, ball cap, and heavy denim coat. You walk back outside and whistle for Speedy. When the dog comes, you open the passenger's door, and the beagle jumps in, ready for Stewart's Sand and Gravel, just a mile down. On the way, big Gradalls are clearing out magnolias and forsythias and most of what you had planted before freeways, now along the four-lane. Some oil companies are looking for natural gas, you've heard.

At Stewart's, past piles of chipseal, you park near the weigh station. Some worker waves you to the burning coal. You get out of your truck, and a blond-haired babyface in his forties sits on a front-end loader. You tell him, "Sit still, I'll get it." You don't want any junk and begin to handpick one ton. Not too heavy and not too light. The boy smokes a cigarette and looks at you, you can see, though he could be looking at nothing. You work and fling and end up with a pretty good, cold sweat, your neck tightening up quick, the muscles rolling themselves up into a ball. You take a deep breath, and a slow shot starts just under the base of your skull and spiderwebs out into your upper shoulders like cracked tempered glass in the windshield of an automobile. You lean back, expanding your chest, breathing deep, trying to relieve it, and it eventually subsides.

The boy on the loader takes another drag.

After loading up, you drive to the scale, pay for the coal. One ton should hold them over for a while. A house like Willy Jr.'s wouldn't take more than two and a half tons for the full year. The clerk tells you, "Boy, Mr. August, I'd be happy to be half as healthy as you when I'm in my seventies." Close enough. You head out for Willy Jr.'s house, another mile away.

* * *

At his bungalow atop a big basement, Willy Jr. stands out on his stoop, one hand scratching his mostly bald head, the other on his hip, a dip in his lip, and his glasses sitting on a frayed lawn chair. Still dressed for the wake, he acts surprised when you show up. "Hey, Uncle Jack. Didn't know you'd be so quick with the coal."

"Where's the boys?"

"Let me get them." Willy Jr. calls and they run out. The older one is stick-thin, probably ten or twelve years old, and never says a whole hell of a lot. The younger one is round like his dad and smiley as all get-out. The older boy's shaved head stands stark next to the mop of a bowl-cut on top of the younger one. He is around eight, or maybe less. Willy Jr. asks them, "Is your mother still in her room?" The boys nod and Willy Jr. looks towards you, whispering, "Locked the door." He goes on, out loud now, his hands wiping over his face and forehead. "I don't know if she's gone clear crazy or what. It's been tough on the boys. I suppose she just needs time."

"Can't blame her. Christ, she ain't no dummy. Four men standing out here ready to shovel coal." You grin at the boys. "She says to hell with these suckers."

The boys look to the ground and grin, too.

"Oh hell, you just don't understand, Uncle Jackie," Willy Jr. says. "Also, I need to tell you," he goes on, retrieving his glasses from the lawn chair and putting them back on, "I probably won't be of much use, on account of my injury."

You get the shovel from the side of the truck and drag it through scattered gravel and dust as you walk to the gate of the bed. It scrapes against cracked concrete slabs that used to be a sidewalk, almost grating to your ear. You pull down the gate, toss the shovel in, hoist yourself up, and get to it, forcing a pile of number six onto old, flat-head steel. You don't glance again at Willy Jr., bent and watching, before you start to shovel the coal down the chute and into the cellar.

As you work, Speedy jumps up on either boy and they follow him from the house, coaxing him away from a loose rooster, just outside the small coop you built for Willy Jr.'s dad. Your nephew has painted an American flag on the side of the coop. In between shovelfuls, you see Speedy chase the boys around a '72 Pontiac, windows busted, sitting on blocks. You found that for Willy Sr. years ago for four hundred dollars cash.

Willy Jr. stumbles about and continues in an explanation about how, naturally, he would help if he could, of course.

"Your mother said you're on compensation now. That right?" You probably have not been to the place since you last shoveled coal into the cellar. The last time, Willy Jr. wasn't home.

"Yes. Checks started coming last month. Finally." Something like life wells in Willy Jr.'s moss-colored eyes now, matching those of both his sons. "Boy, I had one heck of a time." He's worked in the offices at United Machine, worked there since he finished high school, taking calls, pushing pencils. So really, he's never *worked* a day in his life.

"So, what the hell's the matter with you anyway?"

"Oh, I got it in the back"—

"By God, I knew it. Knew it right away. I saw you hobbling around at that service for Norman. I said to myself, that guy's got a bad back. No two ways about it."

"Oh my, Uncle Jackie, you wouldn't even believe it. Some days, I can't even manage to get my pants up." He's whispered this last part.

"Jesus Christ. No wonder that woman of yours locks herself away."

"I mean it. I'm barely able to get out of bed."

"Knew it right from the get-go. That guy's got a bad back."

Shoveling coal into a cellar is not bad work, even for an old man like you. Gravity is on your side. The truck bed is backed up to the house, lifted up. You fill your shovel, and with a quick toss and turn, it gets delivered to the basement of the house. Not like real work, not even close. Really, one ton of coal is a one-man job. Willy Jr. has brought the lawn chair from the stoop, and for much of the time that you shovel, Willy Jr. blabbers on, more sorrow pouring from his thin lips: symptoms, limitations, doctors' warnings. Speaks about a chiropractor, about vertebrae, about some car accident from fifteen years ago. You *uh-huh* and shovel, *uh-huh* and shovel, until most of the coal is down the chute.

When you finally finish up, you step out of the bed and ask, "How 'bout a glass of water, Bad Back?"

Willy Jr. gets up from his chair, laughing you off, and moves quickly. He's back in a minute, hands the glass, clinking with ice, and speaks low. "Thanks, Uncle Jackie. I really mean it. I wish I could pay you for the coal, but I just started getting the compensation from United and Nancy's unemployment could run out anytime now." He shifts his weight. "Oh, do I hurt. Having a hard time even standing here. Feels like someone's turning a screw driver right between my ribcage. Anyway, we've got so much of the credit cards to pay off. I wish I could offer you something."

"It's nothing." Your neck and shoulders and upper and lower back are about to explode outwards, but you walk away, shovel in hand to return to the side of the bed, and nearly trip over a wire that has fallen from the side of the house. "What in the hell is that?" you ask.

"Oh, sorry, Uncle Jack. That connects the satellite. Let me get that out of your way."

"Here, let me see that." You hold the long cable and then go to the cab, retrieve your toolbox, knowing you got some thick wire and black tape in there somewhere. You get it figured out, securing it up on the siding. Who the hell cares if they watch T.V.? What else are they going to do with their time?

"Come and say goodbye to your uncle, boys," Willy Jr. calls. They run back and Speedy follows.

You pull out your billfold and give each boy a dollar bill.

The younger one asks, "Can I have one with a different picture?"

The boy's father grabs him by the wrist and shakes his arm, blasting out an authoritative bellow. "That's enough. What the hell I tell you about your elders?"

"Thank you, Uncle Jackie," they both say, the little one mostly mumbling.

You exchange each for fives. "Tell your dad you ain't no dummies either. You boys got salt in your zucca. Either of you boys play an instrument?" They shake their heads and you walk back towards your truck and whistle for Speedy.

Willy Jr. says, "Wait, Uncle Jackie." You don't. Willy Jr. then motions to the older boy. "Show Uncle Jackie what we got you." The boy runs up to the house, and his father looks back to you. "We got him a set—an early Christmas gift, I guess. Bow season started, but we haven't been out this year. I figure he can practice on the target for now." You stand still when you see the target, twenty yards off, standing upright, a brown field of dust and hay and trash its backdrop. It's next to a small pole flying the American flag, either at half-mast or just drooping. On the target, glued by hand and bright in the sun, stares the first black president-elect of the United States, a big mustache scrawled on his face. Willy Jr., pasty and hunched, brims at his craftsmanship. "Teaching the boy to shoot straight." He's full up of a righteous pride, chest out, probably tickled pink. He knows how you and his mother still vote. He thinks this is fun and games.

The younger one smiles ear to ear, saying, "That's the guy who dresses up like the president."

This is what it has come to.

You feel heavy in your boots, weighted down. There is really nothing else to do now but wrap your hand like a vice around your nephew's shoulder. Standing right next to him and staring outwards, you squeeze your teeth together tight.

There's no hair on your tongue. You tell him, "Thought you were a union man like your dad."

Willy Jr. goes a little limp at first, then tense, but says nothing as you walk through whipping wind, grabbing the target and dragging it back to the bed of your truck.

You load your toolbox into the cab and call for Speedy. As you back out, you roll your window down and holler to the boys as the older one runs out the screen door with his bow in one hand and an arrow in the other. "Remember, come up to the house," you say, "when you have some time tomorrow." Dusk is turning to night, and you tell Speedy, "Let's get the hell out of here, buddy."

* * *

At mid-morning, Willy Jr. brings his sons to your house. They come in through the side door, never locked. "The boys are anxious to see what you got to show them, Uncle Jackie."

"Good enough," you say. "Let's go, boys." You pat Willy Jr. and say just to him, "Let's give that piano a look-see."

"Piano? If it's all the same, Uncle Jackie, I'll rest here awhile. The three of you go off. Mom made some gnocchi. I set it on the table when we come in." He turns fully towards you and says low, "I'm a little leery about them tramping around that old house, if *that's* what you have in mind. And they shouldn't go far, on account of the cold."

You tell him it is just over the hill, before the bog. You look at the boys and say, "Come on."

"Make sure that you button your jackets," Willy Jr. tells his sons.

The boys follow you, their great-uncle. On the way out, the older boy eyes the twelve-gauge shotgun, posted in the corner, straight up, barrel pointing to the ceiling at the top of the stairwell. "Come on now, just a short walk," you tell them.

Speedy, loose, joins and you stop at the garage for a hacksaw, hanging from a nail. You then walk past the rhubarb and along the barbed wire towards the farmhouse. The boys fight with each other, their voices rising and their heads snapping at each other. They fight mostly in sharp whispers, though, as if for you not to notice.

*　*　*

You walk them around the house. The front door remains chained and shut. You hand the older one the hacksaw and lift the smaller boy to the side window, up high. The boy wipes the glass and presses his face against it. "Look up top, if you can. That's a player piano, a hundred years old probably." You motion for the older one to look inside, too, and switch them off. "Look at that brass," you tell them. "Your great-grandma used to play the organ at Mass, you know that? Learned by ear, back where our people come from."

"Who?" the little one asks.

The older one, holding the sill on his own, looks in and asks, "Where's the stairs to the top?"

"What's that, buddy?" you ask.

"The stairs is missing. They're gone."

You set the little one down to the ground and take another look yourself. There is no longer a standing staircase. By God, if these little shits aren't right. You look as best you can, but you can't see one inside. You must've missed this before.

"How we gettin' in?" the older one asks, as his little brother wanders in little circles, singing some cartoon song to himself and pretend-shooting.

"We're not," you say. "Not if there's not a staircase. How do you think we are supposed to get up there? Take a hell of a ladder."

You let yourself down and put your hand on the older boy's shoulder, saying, "Not today anyway, but we'll get to it before long. Let's get out of here, Willy, see if Speedy can find us a rabbit." They begin to move away from the house. You lead and the boys follow, as Speedy sniffs dried dirt.

"That's sassafras, good for walking sticks," you tell them, pointing up ahead to the left.

"What about the deer you told Dad about?"

"Yeah, can we see the dead deer, Uncle Jackie?"

"The hell you want to see something like that for?"

"It's dead, Dad said, big antlers."

"Big antlers, huh?"

You follow the beagle. The boys are quiet mostly. "Watch the poison," you tell them. "It's a real bastard." The little one begins a rambling account of catching poison ivy the summer before. You yep-yep back at his story all the while but stop when you can see the buck.

"Wow," the younger one interrupts himself. Just a day since you saw it first, it's settled into the earth, looking like it hadn't ever been anywhere else. Both boys take off towards it. The older one begins to hold a make-believe bow in his left hand and shoot arrows with his right, biting down hard.

"Your father says you're going to be a hunter," you say. "Have you been out yet, with your bow and arrow?"

"No, not yet. Just target practice."

The younger one begins to shoot pretend arrows, too, and says, "Dead! Dead! Dead!"

You watch them: brothers, rambunctious, all pepper. Tutti pepe. The older boy comes back and grabs towards the hacksaw, asking, "Can we get the antlers?"

"What do you want antlers for?"

"Put them on the wall."

"Yeah," the little one says. "We could put them by the Xbox in our room."

Their great-grandmother, your mother, may as well have been playing a funeral tune. Not for them, though.

"Why not?" you say. "Why the hell not?" You bend down to the buck, your knees feeling their age, or close to it. You lift its head by its antlers with your left hand, and with your right, you place the saw to dead bone. "Why the hell not?" You begin, but the little boy stops you, smacking your shoulder with a small, fat hand.

"Uncle Jackie," the boy asks, "can we get the whole head? Dad has one up in the T.V. room."

The older boy looks at you, too, eyes wide and pleading. "We can let it rot down to the skull."

You release the antlers from your grip, setting the buck's head to the ground, which will be frozen before long, and look them both over. They wear just shirtsleeves under their open jackets; the younger's has space aliens and lasers while the older boy's shows a big Statue of Liberty, saying, ONE NATION UNDER GOD. They are Willy Jr.'s American sons. "All right, buddy," you say. "Tell you what, let's just take the whole goddamn head."

You and your great-nephews take turns sawing at the buck's neck. Back and forth and back and forth, until the entire head is severed from the body, the boys youthful and eager and determined, you seven months shy of your eighty-sixth birthday.

Blood Relations

The biggest crucifix you've seen in recent memory, outside of a church, belongs to Jose, a Mexican, whose new auto-body shop is near Trenton Avenue on the West Side of Uhrichsville. This garage used to belong to someone by the name of Wilson, but you'd never been in, and never knew anything about Wilson. This is on the *far* west side of town. Since Moon, the cousin you'd given all your automotive work almost your whole life, is dead and gone and there are garages everywhere, you've felt like you're out floating and you dock up just about anywhere when you need work to be done.

Where to even start? This place, Wilson's old shop, now Jose's, is as good as anywhere. What's the difference?

Someone had broken the passenger's side glass in your International when you were parked at Argento's Grocery. The doors were unlocked, but the glass was smashed. You'd duct-taped up a thin-plastic garbage bag over it, but Helen's been on you to go have it replaced. Someone your age shouldn't be driving with an open window like that. It's the second time someone's broken in and tried to steal nothing worth stealing from your dump truck, leaving you with a greater financial burden in glass replacement. They'd stolen whatever was in your glove box, which could've been nothing, far as you can tell. One-hundred dollars and Jose could do it right away. No waiting, no haggling, just one Ben Franklin for the job.

You make it there and see most of the writing is in Spanish, some of which is close to your language, and you see Jose eating Spanish food, see his guitar in the corner of his shop, see the television playing a Spanish program, see Jesus Christ hanging by his wrists.

You're here for glass replacement, you tell Jose.

"Yes, yes," he says. "You called earlier, yes." He looks at his plate, half-eaten, and says, "But first, the lunch," in a sort of, *If that's okay with you, my friend?* He is sincere, though, and wants you to rest here. "Are you hungry?" he asks.

"Finish up, buddy. I'm fine." He watches more of the television, laughs at what is on it, finishes his food quickly now, wipes his hands, and then shakes yours. "My friend, the passenger's window, yes?"

"Someone smashed it early yesterday morning."

"Sons-a-bitches!" he says. "Heroin's coming through. That's it. They'll steal anything, even from a dignified gentleman like you. Yes, I'll help you. I'll help." He moves outside, and though he doesn't say, his movement suggests you follow and stay close while he fixes the glass, so you do.

He looks the truck over. "What year is this?"

"Hell, probably '72, the body. Who knows about the rest?"

He begins to nod more and more, becoming more assured, it seems, that he can fix it up, no problem, and making sure you know he can fix it up, no problem. He says, "1972," and brings out a shop vac from his garage and opens the rear door. He wears white overalls and has an impressive mustache, like Papa's. He begins to sweep it all out and crawls around your vehicle, all over the seat, saying "1972" some more. You stand nearby, and try as best as you can to stay out of his way, though he never would have imposed, never would have suggested such a notion, that you were in the way.

He comes back out. "It's a Loadstar," he says. "1700. Big-hauling. These are good trucks, my friend. Rear axle, serious business. These are good trucks."

"1600," you correct him. "And you're goddamn right."

"What's that?" he asks.

"It's a hell of a good truck."

"Yes, of course. By the way, you know what year I was born?" he asks.

"1972?" you say.

"1972," he says and nods.

"You know what year I retired?" you say.

"1972?" he asks.

"No, no, a little later on, five, ten years. Who the hell knows, buddy. Put it this way, I know Reagan was on his way in and I was still working, but not long."

Jose grins. "Did you vote for Mr. Reagan?" Jose asks.

"Hell no," you tell him.

"What year were you born?" he asks.

"Buddy, you wouldn't believe me if I told you."

He works more and asks if your wife is still living.

"No," you tell him, "never had one. You?"

He sets the hose of the shop vac down and says, "I was married *five years*. To the same woman!" He makes himself laugh, heartily. "Now," he says, "I've been divorced six years. I win!" He sweeps out the remaining glass remnants, finds a flat-head screwdriver, pops off the inner paneling, uses a ratchet, sweeps out the rest of the glass inside the door, and goes to a busted-out Dodge Aires K sitting caddy-corner to his garage. He goes inside of it, moves a couple things around, and brings back a new window wrapped in card-board and tape.

When he comes back to your truck, he takes a razor from his hip pocket and begins to cut open the box. "A woman," he says, "is crazy. You know this, my friend?"

"Sure, sure, I know it," you tell him.

"And a divorced woman is crazy like a lion," he says. "Como un leon," he says to himself, shaking his head and laughing.

"Where are you from?" you ask him.

"Far away from here. Mexico City. You know Mexico City?" he says.

You nod and tell him you've heard of it, sure.

"Close, close. But in the countryside."

"When did your people come up here?"

"Late '80s, very long time ago. I was just a kid. I crossed the border, as they say, to California and lived there fifteen years."

"Never been," you tell him. You tell him about a mine foreman who'd avoided the draft because of a bad shin—some baseball accident—and who'd later moved out there and worked as an electrician. "How'd you get over here to Ohio?" you ask.

"I told you: divorce!" He has said it loud and then says, "She still does not know I'm here. She cannot find me, but she's looking still, I know, and when she does"—he raps your old chest with the backs of his fingers softly—"Adios amigo! She will kill me."

He tells you to have a seat, really, and starts to put the pane of glass in the door. You lean on the truck as he puts it back together, only pausing to yell in Spanish at a young

man who pulls up briefly and seems to be apologizing for
something.

*   *   *

After he's all done, he tells you, "Guatemalan, that boy was
Guatemalan. Mountain dialect, old Indian language. I can
get by with it, I can talk to those people, but only since I've
been in Ohio, believe it or not. That's where I learned it.
My people speak Spanish."

"Those people are all Guatemalan?" You roll your window
up and down by hand, admiring his work.

"On the West Side, yes. Very few Mexicans around here,
my friend. Just the business owners." Jose laughs hard, his
small belly shaking, and at the end hits your chest again.
"Probably a cousin of mine, but you have to go back a thou-
sand years. They'll work hard, the Guatemalans," he says.
"Gut chickens, sweep floors, whatever you need. They'll do
it, but then they'll vanish. I paid two of them to shovel all
the snow and chip the ice from out front here, from there
to there, maybe two winters ago when it was bad out. I
used to drag it with that old tractor over there. That Massey
Ferguson. Come to think, it's a '72 also."

"What's wrong with the tractor?" you ask.

"Nothing. I just couldn't keep twisting my back like that,
and besides, they needed the work. They made it look like
summer had come. Really, I mean it. Paid them fifty each.
They were brothers. And the snow comes again, and I can't
find them. Gone." He slides his right hand off his left fast,
motioning to somewhere out there.

"At one time this was all Irish," you tell him. "Several
generations in, so American by then. The whole West Side,"
you say. "And you know how you could tell the American
homes from the foreigners?"

"How's that?" Jose asks.

"The flowers. The Americans planted big beds with lots of flowers."

"Your people didn't have any gardens?" Jose asks.

"Oh, we had gardens, buddy. Hell yes, we had gardens," you tell him.

"What was in them then?"

"Tomatoes, peppers. Beans, lettuce."

"Of course, of course," Jose says.

"Mama said that's how she knew we were settling in," you say, "when her boy started planting trees and flowers all over—wasting manure on flowers—like an American."

"Sounds like my mother," Jose says. "She is miles and miles away. I haven't seen her since I left, but she'll never leave me." He holds his hand to his heart and pulls a picture from his wallet, his hand shaking while presenting it to you. Maybe the homeliest woman you've ever seen. You must furrow your brow, or something. "She's ugly, I know," he says and laughs. "My father," he says, "died long before that."

Jose gets a couple white towels and a bottle of Windex. He starts cleaning your driver's side window. "Guatemalans have changed this neighborhood, let me tell you. I know they're no different than you or me, the Guatemalans," Jose says. "I know this. I am not ignorant. And I know it's strange for foreign people like you or me to complain about other foreign people. I know this." He moves on to the windshield. "Like I said," he goes on, "I am not ignorant."

He wipes down your headlights now and then throws the towel he's been using over his shoulder and takes off his hat, thick, matted hair on top, and wipes his forehead with the back of his forearm. "Here's what I do know, though: I own my own home, two stories. It's 100 years old, or more, my home, but I've updated it, kept it clean and welcoming. I painted it myself last summer and sealed the driveway. I have blacktop. Go see it. It's three blocks away from here." He stretches his arm out and points like he's directing traffic. "All it takes is for one Guatemalan to move in on one side of you and one to move in on the other side. That's it. And if there's one, there's ten. And they shit on the floors. And then guess what?"

"What?" you ask.

"My home is worth nothing. It hasn't happened yet to me, but I've watched it happen and I figure it won't be long. The big businesses love the Guatemalans. The chicken farmers—the ones really eating off those farms, I mean—they love them. But just wait."

"Why's that?"

"They're organizing. They'll get a union, get their papers." He crawls up into the back of your dump truck and starts wiping down the rear window and doesn't say anything for a minute.

Finally, you say, "Then see how long the chicken farms want to keep them around," and laugh. "That new priest over at the church is helping them, somebody said."

"Leading the crusade," Jose says and comes back down.

You say, "See, two dollars an hour, that's fine when they first get here."

He says, "Under the table. Then maybe they get enough leverage to demand an American minimum wage, still off the books. That only works so long. Don't forget, their children, like mine and yours, end up American citizens, and they are on the books. And they'll buy commodes."

You ask him about his children.

He pauses awhile and comes back towards you. "I had a son, but I only have nephews and nieces now. My brother's son is in college," he says. "Right now. Going to be an x-ray technician. Don't take long."

You ask him where.

"Texas," he says. "I told him my only good advice: never get married. And if you do, never to anyone south of Mexico. Probably same blood as ours, but it's not worth it. Let someone else assimilate them. You were what? A railroader? A steelworker?"

"Coal miner, and clay too. We dug it all. If they could burn it or fire it, we dug it, buddy."

"You mined coal when coal mining was hard, my friend. Coal miners live near me, a father and son. They drive an hour towards the Ohio River for the deepmines. Every morning, but it's all machines now."

"Hell, I wish we'd had machines," you say. "Would've been a hell of a lot different, I can tell you that."

"Progress!" Jose says.

"Something like that, buddy."

You head back into the garage and pay Jose, one-hundred, cash, that big crucifix looming over you, dried palm leaves wrapped around it, and he tells you about his other services, oil changes, tire rotations, and so forth. Glass replacement is his bread and butter, but he'll do everything else. Bring it in anytime. He knows you probably don't travel far, but he's happy to be here for you when you need it.

You head out, all your truck's windows so spotless it doesn't even seem like there is glass there at all.

The Washing of Rebirth

The Progress of Man

or The Damming of Il Fiume Noce

It would've been just a couple years before the War when they'd started construction and more than a decade to finish it up. Cousin Moon went over to work on it in 1947, just a few years after he went back the first time, after half a million Italians and a quarter-million Austrians got shot or blown up or gassed out or set on fire. Nobody probably kept track of how many Tyroleans, southern or northern, which wouldn't have made a hell of a lot of difference when they're all dissolving into the mud.

There are two big pictures on the cover of *The Cincinnati Inquirer*'s October 19, 1947, *Pictorial Magazine*. Some cousin of somebody had sent this up here to Moon. Under the first image is a caption about more concrete and reinforcement of steel to keep the whole thing from falling in on itself. In ink pen, a circle is drawn around one of the workers hauling buckets, big rolling carts full up of concrete, from some place to another. The circled worker has a cap, no shirt sleeves, and bunched up pants tucked into his boots. He's got both arms on the cart, which had been lowered from the top of the gorge, according to the caption. Next to the worker is written ME. Around the sleeveless arms, bulging out, is an arrow pointing to this: BORROWED THESE FROM CHARLES ATLAS. Next to the worker Moon claimed he was, is another guy standing still, same outfit, but with long sleeves, one hand in his pocket, the other hanging free. This guy is staring straight on like he knows he's getting his picture taken. You can't make out his face. He is circled with the same ink pen. It says, SOME RELATION OF OURS. Under that, it says, GOT KILLED.

The paper said it had started before the War, the construction, but they got it done mid-century, the highest dam in all of Europe. Fifty stories up from the gorge of Val di Non, six-billion cubic feet of water, five-billion lire, and pushing out two-hundred and fifty-million kilowatts, lighting up the Non Valley like Christmas lights, letting the Tyrolean people in on the Twentieth century.

How many of your people died getting that dam built up?

Off to the left of these images of the great progress of man is an advertisement. It says AMERICA'S SLIP SWEETHEART. Underneath is a drawing of a slim young girl, pin-curled hair and high heels, telling everybody, "If you haven't as yet met MISS YOUTH FORM—the newly patented *straight* slip that has glamour, beauty, and always behaves—there's a real treat in store for you." It says NOW AVAILABLE IN NEW LONG LENGTHS. It says, TRY, SEE, NOTICE, PROVE. It says it's THE ARISTOCRAT OF SLIPS, and you're all in luck because it's on sale.

Moon wrote by that young girl's face, same ink pen: LOOKED ALL OVER. NEVER FOUND HER.

The river Noce, which Papa knew well, which Mama knew well, used to flow free, full of brown and marble trout, undisturbed, through Val di Non, from north of Cles, on down south past Mezzocorona. It's there still but diverted, and valves and floodgates and concrete and steel beams have transformed the Non Valley. They started running apples out of there, even before they dammed up the Noce, and people have made a hell of a lot of money up there in the last century. Relations of yours who've stuck around have made a hell of a lot of money.

Moon said progress was simpler than anybody thought: they just had to get the dam up, most the Agostinis out, the apples growing tall, and the money rolling in.

He wanted the two of you polenta-eaters to go back ten or twelve years ago, to see the house Papa and your zio built, to look down at the dam, at the new lake of Saint Justina, to eat speck and drink red high atop the Dolomites. He would've gone too. What else would you two spend your retirement money on anyway?

You never budged, so the two of you just stayed put, as firm in the earth as the concrete that was poured into the Noce River canyons.

Dago Red

or Here's How Cousin Moon Came to Die

It's 1990-something, and, really, the bed on your dump truck needs to be scrapped, but you've had trouble bringing yourself to replace the whole thing. Wintertime is coming on quick and there are still a number of people, Moon included, in need of burning coal, so you give him a call. "What do you say, gooseneck, can you put 'er back together?" It was Moon who found you the International in the first place. It had cost twelve-hundred dollars by that point, still has the old butterfly hood to this day, and your cousin said he had no need for it himself.

Over the phone, Moon explains the root cause of your troubles has always been loading too many tons into that old two-ton bed. He tells you that you ought to go to a junkyard, find a better bed. But, he'll rig it up, if that's what you want. He'll make it good as new, or "least as good as a twenty-five-year-old, rusted up, coal-hauling dump could be." A pick-and-shovel man, you are not equipped for Moon's line and you know it. You can change oil and brakes and rotors and drop a gas tank. But overhauls, transmission work, anything electrical—these are above your pay grade. All of your business goes to his cousin, a damned good mechanic and a decent man, but you won't catch yourself telling him so.

You never drive the dump over forty miles an hour. Moon warns that if you never take it above second, you'll have transmission troubles, and you'll have one hell of a time ever kicking it into third. You say second is fine, and Moon tells you it is a goddamned waste. But since Moon has stopped driving, it is you who takes him on the occasion that he has some place to go. Usually, it is just a matter of traveling down Center Street, to the bank or the barber or Argento's Grocery. You generally drive down the middle of the street, and Moon about has a heart attack. His ticker isn't too strong to begin with, and while it would be terrible for your cousin to die right in the cab, it might also jolt him enough to keep it going a couple years longer, you figure. Fifty-fifty. You'd take that to the tracks at this age.

Any car comes near and Moon'll start up: "Jackie, better get over. Jackie. Goddamnit, Jack!"

"That's why they call it Center Street," you tell him on those occasions. "They'll get over, buddy, just you watch."

In the wintertime, you may tell Moon something like, "If it's too cold in here, just say, Jackie, it's too cold, and we'll turn up the heat." Moon will tell you it's too cold, and you'll say back, "Eat shit." That's more or less how things go.

None of this ever stops Moon from asking for rides, of course. "I need to pick up my medicine, Jack." "How about some salameats over at Argento's, Jack?" "So-and-so kicked the bucket. Can you take me to his calling hours, Jack?" You always oblige. More recently, Moon has begun to ask for basic handiwork, too—can't make it up a ladder anymore.

* * *

Before you can hang up this time, Moon asks, "Can you patch up the roof? You got time?"

"More time than money. What the hell's the matter with it?"

"Water been coming in, leaking something awful. I don't got enough buckets to keep it."

"Empty one of your goddamned wine jars, why don't you?"

"Bring some shingles, too, if you got 'em."

You hang up and go into your garage to find your tool belt. You know that Moon will be too concerned with the roof to focus on the truck. You'll fix it up for Moon today and get the International to him tomorrow. You don't bother driving. You just call to Ugly, a square-head scent hound, and trek up over the hill, picking your meaty legs up and down through the bog, briers, and gullies that dip from the base and go up again, like you are walking up and down Mama's limestone Alps of Italy's north, a place you've never been.

Moon was born in Europe, of course. He was the eldest of Zio Federico's three children, your first cousin, some years older, and not any bigger than a minute. He'd come over when he was seven and lived on the South Side for almost his entire life, ever since the family docked at Ellis Island and made its way south to the foothills of the Appalachian Mountains. He hasn't been carousing in taverns for decades and spends most of his time these days in his small mobile home, painted tan acrylic latex and blended into the backdrop of a whole lot of nothing, setting not far away from your house, just north of Skunk Hollow. Really, it's a two-bit house trailer with a shingle roof. You're not sure, but Moon had been married at least a couple times. You can't keep straight which women your cousin had just taken up with and which ones he'd ended up marrying. One of them was a war bride who'd run off not long after they came back here, one of them was a local farm girl from Rush, and one, who grew up on Plum Run, even made Moon get religion, you remember. Anymore, the house stays empty except for Moon.

* * *

You make it in no time.

"Where's that vehicle?" Moon calls, standing outside, dressed for the day, holding his ball cap in his hand. He is eating an onion like an apple with his other and has a wild shock of hair that, like yours, has kept its color except for gray here and there and hangs down over a leathered forehead. Now old as hell, seven years your senior, Moon's skin looks like a mail satchel.

"Junked it."

"You what?"

"Worthless piece of shit is why," you say as Ugly pisses on tomato stakes.

You walk into the home and Moon follows back in. The whole place smells damp.

"That's a good truck, Jackie," Moon says behind you, chomping bits of onion.

"Figured I'd leave her for today. Get your roof patched, and you can get to the truck when you got time." You approach one of the buckets in the sunken living room, overflowing, but at a drip's pace, just splashing up a little at a time. You move it with your foot, spilling some onto the coarse carpet, faded with light and dark green checkers.

"Hell's the matter with you?!"

"All right," you say, "what're we looking at here?"

Moon shows you the ceiling corner.

"Uh huh." You go back outside, passing pink flamingos and the Blessed Mother surrounded by hyacinths. In Moon's small garage you helped him build years ago, you grab a ladder from two hooks hanging above several carboys across from a potbelly coal stove. They're filled up with dago red, and Moon calls it just that. He'll tell anyone who'll listen that he's an *Italian*. You know Moon is close behind, keeping an eye, and tip the ladder towards the six-gallon glass containers.

"Come on now, Jackie, get serious for once in your life, would you?"

You take the ladder out and prop it on the side of the trailer.

Moon tosses what was left of his onion and gathers several shingles that lie in the garage into a wheelbarrow, the old shallow kind with the solid tire. "You don't got no shingles from your place? I don't got too many left, you know."

"Hell, you got more than you know what to do with," you say.

Moon pulls out a pinch of tobacco.

Your face feels like it has been somewhere between a smirk and a squint since arriving, and you grab hold of the shingles and a caulking gun, and climb up. You scoot sideways, settle in. You start to remove the curled shingles with a blade, rip them up and throw them down to a tarp Moon has spread out for you, apply the roofing cement, and take your hammer from your belt. Moon shields his eyes from the bright sun with one hand and tries to direct you with the other. Every once in a while, he bends and pets Ugly.

You go on removing the old and securing the new, and Moon stands on the ground against the ladder, holding onto the base as if steadying it; he is leaning more than anything. His legs aren't good anymore, his left shot during the War, he claims, even though he'd mostly played in the Army band. He's told his stories so much he really believes them. Either way, the last several years, Moon has moved awfully slow.

You hammer one galvanized nail and then another while you keep the one on deck between your teeth. It doesn't take long before you bust your thumb. That you can ignore.

You've always left a little bit of yourself on every job. But then you bend another nail in half. You climb down the ladder, take a block, and place the roofing nail on it. You squat as if you are again in the low mines—you can feel it in your thighs—and hammer the nail until it straightens. You climb back up and finish the job. You tell Moon, "All right, I got to get the hell out of here."

"Want some red? Here, come in here to the garage, Giacomo. When you plan on getting the dump to me?"

You carry the ladder and follow Moon, who sifts through a cardboard box filled with empty two-liter pop bottles. He'd cleaned them out so that he can eventually fill them up and secure them with a screw cap, rather than corking them.

You put the ladder back and say over your shoulder, "Tell you what, gooseneck, I'm fine for now." You start back towards home.

"You sure?" Moon calls.

"Hell yes. That red's no good."

* * *

You drink, but you're no drunk. Even though you were a pick-and-shovel man, and your trade not skilled, you still found it difficult to function after too much drink. There was a time or two you'd really tied one off and had to dig a ditch the next day. Seems everyone who's ever really tied one off had to dig a ditch the next day.

Anymore, give you a glass of red, and you'd never get to anything else for the day. It is something the way Moon, that little bugger, has been able to work on an automobile after drinking a quart or two. There'd been times in Moon's prime, you were sure of it, that he stayed out all night with no sleep and spent the following day rebuilding engines, switching out worn clutches. It's really something.

In school, Moon had been studious, could've made a good teacher. He had his nose in books written in English, history mostly, for most of his boyhood, but never made it out of the seventh grade. He worked in coal mines for a few years, in the Rosemarie, in fact. Even before the explosion, it wasn't worth his life, he told you. From the way he complained, it would have seemed like there were no saints in Heaven that could have kept Mirocleto Agostini down below. But he stayed a good while before taking shifts at the West End filling station. Then, after both your dads got killed, he was on at the sewer pipe for a time, and eventually, he played accordion for Patton's Army. You didn't see your cousin for two years during the Second World War.

Overseas is where Moon took up his trade. Gave up repairing instruments and started repairing automobiles, anything mechanical. This was probably the most useful thing Uncle Sam did for anyone in the Agostini family. And he was even back and forth to Europe after the War. Then sometime years later, Moon did end up teaching, working with youngsters at the Ohio Valley Vocational School. Truth is, when he was sober, Cousin Moon could've found work most anywhere. Had he wanted, he could've torn a car completely apart and put it back together, like that. He knew his goddamned chickens. Moon was always interested in how things worked. To you, if they worked, they worked.

* * *

The next evening, you and Ugly head down your gravel drive, up and over the hill, and up to Moon's. You about hit his mailbox, park, and watch your cousin hobble from the door, coming down from or falling into some kind of bender. You leave the keys on the seat and step out of the cab. With one hand in your hip pocket, you size up your cousin. Moon's eyes are pink and off somewhere else; he sways just enough to make *you* dizzy.

"Damn it, Moon, I don't know that I ever find you when you're not half-pigeon-eyed," you say.

"Finally brought her over, huh?"

"Look at yourself."

"Give it a rest. I drink it at my meals, that's all," Moon says.

"Moon, why the hell you spend every dime you got drinking and carrying on?"

"What the hell you talking about?"

"Don't bullshit me. If your nose was any redder, you could serve it with shortcake."

"A glass of vin. That's what's good to me. If anyone has anything to say about it, he can go fly a kite." Moon puts his hands up, sort of like a kite, and nearly falls over.

You say he looks like a television preacher.

"Jackie," Moon says, "want this fixed up or not?"

"You can't handle this job like you are, you goddamn dummy. When's the last time you even handled a shovel?"

"Hell you talkin' about, shovel?"

"How 'bout a woman?" Fact is, it has been a good ten years since either of you has handled a woman. Maybe twenty. Who knows?

"Eat shit. You want the damned old dump fixed or not?"

"Yeah, go ahead. If I'm going to haul a goddamned thing, it'll need fixed."

Moon eyeballs the truck. "Damn it Jackie, you need to take better care. I'd have never found her for you if I knew she was going to end up like this. This is a good truck." Childless like you, your cousin has come to admire others' automobiles the way fellow parents might genuinely compliment the handsomeness or beauty of another's child, even if the child is not really good-looking, but because it makes them think of their own children. It makes them think of other times.

"Christ, you smell like groundhog piss, Moon."

Moon says he is just a little sick and walks back towards his screen door. "This coming week sometime, anyway. I'll get to it."

You go to the garage. Several sawhorses sit with a flat board across them. On top are large wine jars, four in all. Two are close to full, one nearly empty, and the last clear of anything but the remaining sediment. Moon has seldom paid for booze thanks to the grapes on his own arbor. His dago red is a grade above any made by the other old-timers on the South Side or over on Grant Street, and you admit to yourself it is damned good. Moon even brews beer, or used to, grew his own hops, but Ohio's barely good enough for grapes.

Near the sawhorses are a couple or three crates of homebrew. Most of the bottles have not been touched, though a few are busted out, and cobwebs are spread between the bottlenecks. More or less, the homebrew is for company, though Moon has few visitors. When you were kids, Moon used to watch your fathers rake and bottle the red, which they'd drink every meal. Sometimes, Moon had been allowed to help separate the grit and dregs out. You never cared one way or another and just helped with the hog at butchering time.

You go back into the trailer. "That red's nearly gone. Never dry for a minute, huh cugino?"

"Oh, Jesus, calm the hell down. I'll get to your truck I said." Moon lies on a brown, wood-trimmed davenport.

"You ought to do away with that business." You go into the small kitchen and drink several big gulps of water from the tap, almost a dipper-full each with your cupped hands. You wipe your face and point right at Moon. "You're going to dry out awhile, understand?"

"You remember Zio Luciano ever drinking water? Never, not once do I remember your father having a glass of water. During prohibition, no less."

"Papa was no lush"—

"And if I recall," he goes on, "wasn't it you who drank the kerosene out of your headlamp?"

You ignore this last accusation. That was a long time ago.

"Table wine's one thing," you say. "That's what Papa drank. You're gonna dry out." Truthfully, some people will never be able to shake themselves from it, to take care of themselves, and the only thing you can do, what you've got to do, is look after them, is love them.

You plop into an armchair and ask Moon how long ago he bottled this last batch.

Moon looks up, points nowhere in particular with two fingers, and says, "Two, three—hell I don't know."

You throw two of your own fingers and holler, "Cater."

Moon sits all the way up while throwing his fingers back at you, showing four in all, calling, "Sèt," while you flash two again, saying, "Òt."

You call more but neither of you wins. You continue for three or four minutes, louder and louder like the old days, before you get up and move towards the door.

"I'm taking your Ford home with me."

"Have at it. You ought to stick around, though. Mayberry's coming on," Moon says, pointing over to an old black and white set. "Picture don't come in no more, but I get to listen while tinkering around."

The flatbed hasn't been moved in who knows how long, and a sticker on the rear bumper reads: DEMOCRAT AND PROUD. You whistle for Ugly to jump in, turn the key several times to give her some juice, get the fuel pump humming, and drive away.

* * *

At home, you go to your own garage and find a cut hose and several five-gallon plastic buckets with lids; they have steel handles and had once been filled with plaster, but are good and clean now. You take them to the side of the house and hose out daddy long-legs once more for good measure. You put them in the Ford's bed and don't even stop inside to take a piss before driving back to Moon's.

It is eleven o'clock. You lift the handle on the garage door, push it all the way up. You go in, find the homebrew braced up on a bench made of old two-by's and start stacking the crates in the back of the flatbed. Rather than carry off the bulky, glass carboys, you instead stick the hose down in, get it started with your mouth, and siphon all of the dago red into the more manageable buckets, leaving the empty jars in place.

You cap the buckets and put it all in the bed, securing it as best you can with a length of chain. You go inside and Moon is out, choking on his own snores. You throw a wool blanket on your cousin. Moon would never ask for payment, but you leave a hundred-dollar bill on a small oak table next to the arm of the davenport.

You start home in the pickup. There are old canisters of Gojo cleaner and torn-up washrags all over the place in here. Already, the weather is turning something terrible and Moon's got one working wiper. Come Christmastime, you'll all freeze to death if Moon doesn't fix up that dump so it can haul coal.

After you park, you take the beer and wine down your own cellar steps and leave them at the base. You take two bottles of homebrew upstairs, open them up with a lobster-shaped bottle opener somebody gave you for a gift sometime, and drink both fast, leaving the bottles to leak the remaining foam into your kitchen sink. It hits you hard before you finally fall asleep.

* * *

Monday comes around and you haven't heard back, so you figure you'll drive the flatbed out again. You take a poppy seed cake Helen has fixed for you, which is damned good, and her date pudding with small marshmallows, which you don't care for, in a paper sack. You take both, along with a new bag of candied orange slices, call for Ugly, and head to Moon's.

When you arrive, you park next to your International, not moved, and figure you ought to say something to Moon about the axel on the Ford's driver's side. You can hear a clicking and think it might need a replacement. Also, the clutch has been slipping. Ugly stays lying in the cab.

You knock on the door and turn the knob at the same time. "Moon," you call, "Santy Claus's got some goodies for you, buddy."

There are no lights on inside. You set the sweets down by the front door. You walk into the second room of the trailer. Moon is curled sideways, dead on the floor, and you know it right away. You've seen dead before. His eyes are almost opened, his face bloodied and bandaged with a half-assed tourniquet, and the body's fresh rot masks the must and mildew of the place. The receiver from his rotary telephone lies off the hook near his hand; bloody fingerprints run along the length of its black plastic neck. The oak table sits in the center of the room with your one-hundred-dollar bill still on top, undisturbed. At the corner, where Moon's face must've smashed, blood has dried the color of rust.

He's gotten into booze again, somehow or another, and killed himself, goddamnit.

You kneel down. Moon's skin is cold and his undershirt is caked with what looks to have once been runny vomit, tobacco leaves, and blood. Seems like he's shit himself, too. There is no telling how long Moon has lain in his own mess. You stand and turn on the lights. Except for a lot of blood, the nearly bare trailer is like it had been a couple days before. You brush your hands against your pant legs and walk outside, breathing in and widening your eyes, feeling the air hit them, feeling like you've had a few cups of coffee all of a sudden. You step into the garage and find it like you've left it, too. There is no trace of homebrew and no dago red inside any of the carboys.

You brace your arms on one of the sawhorses and look at the cement. It is clean enough, the whole garage as well-kept as it has ever been. You stand inside for what might be a while or no time at all, surveying a sea of wrenches and ratchets and sockets spread out over a workbench. A topless calendar from 1962 is pinned to the wall, the edges brown and curled in, and a world's almanac with a beat-up hardcover lies open beneath, face-down.

You start to grab one of Moon's wrenches, but stop and look close towards the bottoms of the jars. They've been emptied all right, cleaned out. Cousin Moon—the closest thing you'll ever have to a big brother—must've eaten every last bit of red sediment.

The Washing of Rebirth

or Did Cousin Moon Kill Somebody?

Yes, two people, but not in the War, and nobody remembers anyway, so what's the difference?

This was in 1932, end of Prohibition. Moon had been helping out at a filling station owned by a Greek named Katsaros, who also owned the West End restaurant, where Moon had bussed tables.

Antifreeze is used in automobile radiators, the papers said, to keep things cool and running. This was 1932, don't forget, not everyone knew. A lot of the old-timers, especially foreigners like your people, didn't even drive. Antifreeze tastes sweet, goes down easy, and can kill stray cats quick. Like Mr. Salvadori, the Greek was running booze, out of his filling station, and everybody did know that. The cops, everybody. This used to be a wide-open town, remember. They'd deal cards right in the store-front windows.

A taxi driver brought in two good-for-nothings. They wanted booze, one of them an old saloon owner and the other a railroader. The Greek had told Moon to sell them a jug under the counter. He told Moon to charge them twenty-five cents. He told Moon it was antifreeze. He told Moon they'd never come back.

The two good-for-nothings complained about the price, of course, but they looked it over, said they'd never seen any like that before, bluish-green, thick-as-milk. They bought it.

* * *

The papers said, POISON POTION KILLS TWO AREA MEN. The papers said, BOY CONFESSES SALE OF DEATH DRINK. The papers said Cousin Moon violated the state law PRO-HIBITING THE POSSESSING, DISPENSING, OR SELLING OF COMPLETELY DENATURED OR WOOD ALCOHOL WITHOUT THE PROPER LABEL.

When the first guy showed up to the police station, he was soapy-eyed, sozzled-out, canned-up, full-as-a-tick. Arrested on the spot for intoxication, but took ill and died that night at Sisters of Mercy. The other guy, they found after they broke down the door of his living quarters on East Center Street, face-down, dead a while. They arrested Moon that next day. They arrested the taxi driver that next night.

Moon confessed that he sold them the supposed booze. Moon confessed that a coworker from the West End told him he shouldn't have. Moon confessed that the Greek told him to lie to the chief of police, to tell him he never sold any radiator fluid to those two. Moon ended up held in juvenile court.

The county coroner up in Dover, named F.J. Martin, investigated to see if poison liquor was the cause of death. The coroner, F.J. Martin, ran an autopsy and said their kid-neys were seared and ceased operations and then ceased the operations of the rest of the body.

The prosecutor, S.L. Cook, said Moon sold it in good faith. The prosecutor, S.L. Cook, said state law prohibits the possessing, dispensing, or selling of completely denatured or wood alcohol without the proper label, yes, but that just applies to five-gallon wine jars. The prosecutor, S.L. Cook, said the taxi driver couldn't be charged because this was only a quart. Besides, the two dead were drunkards, lushes, boozehounds, didn't drive, couldn't drive. What did they know about automobiles?

* * *

If there's a moral to the story, you figure, it's one of forgiveness. The Greek had shown immeasurable mercy to your cousin, Moon, even though Moon had ratted him out and humiliated him in his written confession. See: the Greek had paid off the prosecutor, S.L. Cook, and the coroner, F.J. Martin, rendered a verdict of accidental death. How can someone show somebody else that much compassion?

Most people bought the story that Cousin Moon didn't know the two men would drink the antifreeze. The papers said, HOMICIDE VERDICT RETURNED. The papers said, CAN'T HOLD AGOSTINI.

Moon was released from custody and the taxi driver never had to pay his own five-hundred-dollar bond.

They sent the saloon owner's body to Wheeling, West Virginia, the other side of the river, his former home, for burial. He was survived by his mother in Bridgeport and his sisters in New Athens. They had a funeral for the other guy at his parents' home on Sixth Street. He was also survived by four older brothers who had moved up to Canton and out to Lorain.

Cousin Moon was sixteen, and it would be more than a decade before he'd see hell on earth in the European theatre.

These were different times, remember.

What's Left When the Whole World Has Packed Up and Gone

What's Left When the Whole World Has Packed Up and Gone

When Willy's boys come over, they like to bring a metal detector. You give them an old garden shovel and a pickaxe. Tell them to have at it back there. They'll dig up the old spikes. There are all kinds of tracks and plates, even whole cars, buried back there, not far underneath the surface, mostly moss. When the mines left, they left, left it all. The boys will get to take a bucket of spikes with them back home. That metal detector *beep-beep-beeps* while they scoot around, getting muddy. You sit up with Speedy and holler down at them, letting them in on the old times, how it all used to be. They generally find several spikes, or whatever, to take back with them. Who knows what all, and you don't know if they are ever quite listening.

You've thought of other things to give them too, from the house, from the garage: your old arrowhead collection, the butterflies you pinned on a big board. Today, you give them the small bricks you made when you were at the sewer pipe. They are burgundy, some single bull-nosed with one edge rounded off, some of them with three holes cored through the tops, and some others yet frogged. You'd made a whole set, now chipped on the edges but mostly intact. Along the headers on each, etched in with your pocketknife, says 1967. Across the stretched faces says JACK AUGUST, CLAY-MASTER.

This was in response to an old German clay worker, a foreigner, who'd told you there he was, a clay worker, a foreigner, and his son was now the postmaster, an American. You can only find three of these bricks and give them all three to the boys. Take 'em, fellas.

When they come to get the boys, Willy's wife tells you that they ought to donate these bricks to the new clay museum they put up on the West Side. It's folk art, she says, what the workers made back in your days. They'd love to have it over there, she says, your folk art. You've given it all to her boys, thinking maybe they'd enjoy playing with it, and who knows if she'll give it away to anyone else? Willy's family wants to know if you want to see the new museum. The boys enjoy it, they tell you. They can make small plates, write whatever they want on them, and then they get to fire them right there, take them home. Commemorative pieces.

Some of the boys from the school went over, some Saturday, Willy Jr. says while the boys sort out their new spikes, and a couple of the boys, along with one of Willy's, spelled out something obscene when they put their plates together, Willy Jr. explains, and the boys got an in-school suspension. Can you imagine that? Willy Jr. asks you. Off school time and off school property, how could they suspend his boy on account of that? It was only mischief, he tells you. He believes in punishment, of course, of blistering their asses when needed, he says, but that's up to him, up to their mother.

Believe him—he takes a drag of a cigarette—their mother was livid. How could their son be so disrespectful? He's been raised better than that, and he knows better. That's their prerogative, though, not some public school's. His taxes pay for that school, for crying out loud. Who are they to punish his boys? Half the time, Willy Jr. and his wife think about pulling the boys out and educating them on their own, she breaks in. Do you know how liberal these schools have become? she says. You ought to see the kinds of things they're teaching them, in science, in health, in social studies. If you saw, Willy Jr. tells you, you'd rethink a whole lot of things. It's liberal all right, he says. It's *gynocentric*, she tells you, saying it like she's unveiling a new, cherished toy somebody gave her. Public education is meant to ruin boys, and he's not afraid anymore to make sure his boys know it either, so that way they can keep their eyes open wide, Willy Jr. says. Probably better to go back to the old country schools, he says, the two-room ones, like you and Willy Jr.'s mother first went to before the Catholic school—*speaking of liberals*, his wife breaks in. Anyway, the city does do a good job with the clay museum, of putting their taxes towards something actually useful, and you ought to see it, they say.

Before St. Theresa's, you'd gone to the Haley school, several classes jammed into a big room. The teacher made you sit under her desk because you couldn't sit still. You made faces at the other kids while she tried to teach and you got your knuckles beaten with a set square, a triangular ruler. To this day, the pinky on your left hand is curved inward, but that could've been the result of a whole lot of things. Your left hand isn't much better, but that got beat, or else tied behind your desk when, naturally, you tried to write with it on the occasion that you tried to do what the teacher asked. There was an American girl in school there named Josephine, curly-haired. Oh, to have curls like that, Helen used to say. You and your sister and Norman would walk with her on your way home. Her mother ran you out of their house because you kicked over their piss pot, on purpose.

Not long after, at St. Theresa's, you and Norman and other boys found a relation of Josephine's in the woods down from the school, dead with his tongue cut out. The nuns beat you for even seeing that.

These were different times, remember.

* * *

Behind where Speedy's box is, where the boys are digging, is full of clay, down beneath. There are flowers, too. You take a St. Anthony's turnip and call the younger one over. He comes along without protest. You hold the buttercup flower under his chin and say you knew this one liked butter. He runs off again and you sit, your ass now wet from the damp grass. Willy Jr. and his wife still ramble on, to each other mostly, but to you, too, and you rip back some growth and put your fingers down in, your other arm draped over Speedy, snoring with his chin on the ground. The mud is thick, it's wet, it smears. Just walk back there and your boots will feel like they're heavy with concrete. You will use a flathead screwdriver to dig it out from the soles when you get back up to the house. Some of your clothes, Helen doesn't even bother with, try as she might, after you've been messing around back here. No amount of Lestoil, she tells you, is going to get this clay all cleaned up, and she sure as hell isn't going to run your clothes, caked like this, through that new Maytag she had them put down in your basement. Not a Maytag, not pairs of pants full of clay. What are you doing back there anyway?

You sit and watch Willy's boys and roll the mud into balls the size of little marbles or the iron ore pellets that used to fly off the rail cars hauling them. You collected and shot those with a slingshot. Willy's wife says something to her husband about just throwing the boys' boots out when they get home. Their feet have just about grown out of them anyway.

There is only one underground clay mine left, over in Stone Creek, five, ten miles from here, off of County Road 21. And up in Amish country and out in Bowerston, they still make brick, by the thousands. That's only two places, though. That's about it, anymore. At one time, they made ceramics and china at dozens of potteries, all kinds of brick plants and sewer pipe, and this was *The Clay Capital* of the whole damn world. Up in East Liverpool, over in Zanesville, and here. Over 30 plants just here alone. The Jacksons make liners for chimney flues now, plastic taking over all the sewer pipe. How many workers do they have there? Less than fifty, if that. And, call it what they want, they're not even Jacksons anymore.

This was it, some operation at one time, the whole world right here. You lived it, and it's mostly gone. The world is fleeting. But they didn't get all the clay, so much just sitting under Speedy's box, as an example, and they won't ever. You don't need a museum to tell you about clay mining.

You take a little pellet you've rolled and pitch it at the older boy. It misses, but you start launching more and he turns and swats at one and looks up at you. His surprised smile takes shape and he starts throwing them back at you. "Get Uncle Jackie!" the little one says. Willy Jr. shakes his head and takes off his glasses. His wife rolls her eyes and crosses her arms, and smiles.

The Souls of the Faithful Departed

On your RCA color set, set atop another set, there is never much of anything on even though there are a whole lot of things on. You've heard others making similar complaints— your sister, even Willy Jr.

Saturdays, they play old Vincent Price pictures in the morning, '50s movies. They've been running cable television to the South Side for thirty years now, and this is good as it gets, you guess. The Vincent Price they have on this morning is about a magician who goes crazy and starts killing people. Starts with the globe turning, shining brightly, like all the old movies do. As if people don't have enough to worry about, day-to-day, they need to watch murder on television. As if we'd never had wars, or cave-ins, or lymphatic cancers. As if people need something else to goose them up. You watch it through, though. Ends with them figuring out the killer by fingerprints, some novelty for those days. Vincent Price was without a pencil mustache in this one, but his clean shave was no match for modernity. A Bob Vila comes on after, and he's putting on big doors to a cellar. Some fella in a red shirt is doing most of the work for Bob Vila, and old Bob is talking up a storm.

There are always preachers on the stations just past this one, and they are generally crying and singing and praising and making money. It's a wonder they stay in business, but it must be lucrative, all those worshippers crying and singing and praising right back at them. Sometimes the preachers are sitting at a desk—call-in shows. These will give you your answers to what ails you, too, to sort things out for you. Is your cancer-ridden great-aunt right with the Lord? No need to get doctored! Is your child a homosexual? Let's all pray they start poking the right way! Will you walk again? Will you be able to sleep at night? They've got the answers right here, you can bet your ass, to the problems that can't be fixed or the problems that aren't even problems. And that's the best way to make money, to act like you know the answers, to be able to look straight into a camera lens and tell people "God is just" or "The meek will inherit the earth" or "Hang the cross-beams between the joists like so" or "Fingerprints on the gun! Fingerprints on the safe! We've got him now!"

You turn the station back to Bob. Hinges here. Line her up straight. Here's how you lock it. And the other fella is busting his ass. Bob Vila has a hell of a job. He's showing off an old coal furnace towards the end, talking about gravity circulation. This is how they used to make them, he's telling you. Bob Vila is a Cuban from Florida, and got educated—had gone on to college and John F. Kennedy's Peace Corps. You've watched him enough to know all this.

* * *

To hell with them. To hell with Bob Vila. You steady yourself up with either hand from a La-Z-Boy you've had an awful long time. It's brown-yellow leather with wooden arms. It sits low to the floor, but it does recline. There are some cat claw markings from some other time on the top part where your head lies back. That was a long-haired, bob-tailed, beautiful cat, but that cat's long dead and the rocker's still rocking. The La-Z-Boy had the last laugh, in other words. Anyway, your legs have fallen half asleep, but you're able to shake them off enough and move towards your own basement. You sort of stumble down the stairs. Several, then a landing by the side door, then ten or twelve more.

In your basement, you have a countertop, a sort of snack bar with four stools, some plastic fruit sitting in a bowl on top of it. That's off to the left. There's a heavy glider with a cushion sort of in the middle that should be on somebody's porch somewhere, a washing machine and dryer where Helen takes care of your clothes once a week, a big double cement washtub with a steady drip next to that, a couple or three dressers along the back wall, and steel poles to hold up the place. It all smells of Lestoil from Helen scrubbing your work pants. There's a big octopus furnace like the one Bob Vila was showing everybody, a coal chute, and a thin coat of black coal dust on most everything. It smells like everything in your life has smelled, sort of like a wet burn, that cellar dust, if that can make sense to anyone anywhere other than here, but how could it?

The basement walls are painted cement blocks, originally white. It was over this past year or so when you started messing around with these old blocks, after they ran natural gas to the house, after Helen told you they were replacing your heat and you stopped shoveling in coal. That's when you started drawing pictures on the walls, trying to raise the dead. You take your fingers and dip them in pooled up water in the double tub and start. You always begin with the noses over the bumpy, chunked-out concrete, with the curve of the bridge, then the nostrils. You round up the foreheads then and make the circle of the head sort of big and fast. This is all fast work. You can adjust that a little more as you go. Now the eyes. Start with their shape is all, then the eyebrows. You always put in the lips last for the face and then straighten out the chin and the jawline. Ears. You use all your fingers to make the hair, however much. Maybe a neck. The whole thing is probably twice the size of a regular head. You run your fingers of each hand down the face on each side.

You press so hard you might as well be carving these into the old wall.

Your mind sort of swirls, sort of turns itself off intentionally once you get going. Could anyone else see them, make any sense of them? To you, and maybe nobody else, this one looks like Moon. Small eyes, big wisp of hair on top. Big ears. Big smile. Small chin that sinks in mostly to the neck. Beneath him is Cousin Norman. Heavy cheeks, squared-off jaw, fat head. Over from him, above, is Mama, but like she looked like when you were a child. Long eyelashes, dark lips. There's Mr. Salvadori, lean and bent-nosed, and Willy Sr., looking like a Polack Humpty Dumpty. Some have bodies even, the first ones, but mostly it's their faces. The long one with the veil is of old Helen Miller, the mother of Felix, who got killed in the Rosemarie blast. Her heart broke in two on the way home from her child's burial service and she died right there on the roadside.

This one now does look like Moon, your dead cousin, and the others look like the dead, too, but the longtime dead and gone, farther back, their faces shining through as white lines cleaned into decades of coal dust, but these will fade too, like everything. There isn't much space left on your wall for new ones, the mural having filled in across the back, up against block windows, rounding up over the curve of a dresser mirror, some small half-faces peaking out from behind it. You dip your wet fingers into some black dust and dirt mixed up on the cement floor. It's thick, all of it, now a wet, sandy sludge, and you add stubble to Moon's face. You can hear him bellyaching. You can hear him bitching at you about dirtying up his face. To hell with you, Moon. So you fling mouse shit on Moon's chin with your fingers now. Fast. What are you going to do about it, Moon? Un, doi, cater, sèt. Morra! Morra! Morra! You start wiping your hands over his whole face until this spot looks as blank and brown as it had before you'd started.

That's when the door bangs up at the top of the cellar steps.

"Uncle Jackie, you home?"

You move quick as you're able anymore, look up, adjust your glasses, and pull the string next to the light bulb off to make the basement black. "The hell you here for, Willy?"

His boys stand behind him. One of them has on a mesh football jersey. The other has on a ball cap. They are holding a wrapped present.

"Coming by to say Happy Birthday."

"Happy Birthday back at you, buddies." You climb up the stairs and try to tuck in your shirt as you walk. "The hell you doing? Playing ball?"

"Yeah," the older one says and looks down.

"Linebacker on the junior varsity. Two-a-day practices," his dad says to you.

You are back into your kitchen and motion for them to come on into the living room, saying to the boys, "Candy's in the top drawer." Another Bob Vila's on and now Bob's in an attic with a housewife talking about insulation, or something.

"Little loud, ain't it, Uncle Jackie?" Willy Jr. laughs towards his boys when he says it. You act like you don't hear and plop down into the old La-Z-Boy. They take their places across your golden-velvet sectional couch, one you'd bought for

Mama. Have you ever even sat down on that couch your-self? It's sat in here, how long? Fifty years? Probably more.

"Is your team any good, buddy?" you ask the boy.

He shakes his head and smiles. "Not really."

"Not yet." His dad points at him and curls up his bottom lip, as if to be serious about the whole matter.

"Who's your coach?"

"Barrett."

"No, it ain't, buddy," you tell him. "Ain't Barrett. It's Ber-etta. They're Milanese. Don't let him or anybody else tell you their name is Barrett. He's no more Barrett than I'm O'Malley, let me tell you."

The boys are looking at the coffee table.

"What about you?" you ask the little one.

"Cartoons," his dad tells you. "That's about it."

"Anime," the boy says.

"What did he say?" you ask.

"He can draw, too," his big brother says.

"Anime," Willy barks loudly, crossing his arms, the way he shouts when he tries to tell you anything and figures you can't hear worth a damn, the way people used to talk to foreign people like your mother and father.

You feel your eyes squint as Willy Jr. moves his eyes from you to his boys and back. You are confident and content in your befuddlement, ornery as all get-out. "Annamae," you say. "You mean Annamae Mancini? She's the middle one."

The boys don't know what the hell you're talking about, and you know that, and you know they know that, and that's the whole idea.

"What the hell you interested in the Mancini sisters for? Little old for you, aren't they? Ugly as sin." They weren't unattractive, but you're having fun here. "Why you think they never married? They couldn't teach you nothing," you tell the boys.

That breaks it open there for your nephews, all three of them, the father and his boys, and you four have one of those laughs you only get to have with your blood, with your own tribe.

Those sisters lived about three blocks from the church, where everybody went when your people started coming to this country a century ago. There was Ester, too, the pick of the litter, and there was another, known by everyone in town as Flash. Of all the ways someone around here might've earned that moniker, Flash had done it the way a Mancini sister would: through her devotion to the one, holy, Catholic, and apostolic church through earnest photographic documentation of every occurrence at St. Theresa's in the decades since post-Vatican II cardinals would open everything up and allow their priests to permit flash photography during Mass. And besides: bologna sandwiches on Friday! What a time to be alive.

Flash had taken pictures of everything that ever happened at the red-brick church house, next to the school, a block from the bank, maybe half a block from the Clay City Pharmacy. She was a modern woman in that sense, and only that sense. You'd be in line for communion with Mama, back when you went still, and Flash would shuffle out, usually in a lilac or green pantsuit, with a small hat, matching, and little glasses. She was a thin woman, frail, and her camera would start clicking and flashing. Who knows where all those pictures ended up? The long and the short of it, anyone will tell you: the Mancini sisters, those three, should've been nuns. Never married, devoted to the daily Mass, devoted in their service to the church. They had a younger brother too, Albie, who drove truck and would wheel his wife into the side of church, the "Amen Corner," where you could fit a chair because there weren't full pews. Annamae, now dead, was the old days really, her and Ester and Flash and Albie and his poor wife—they were remnants of some other place. And it's peeling away at its edges like old paint on basement brick, coming undone.

Willy Jr. starts telling you how he was at Jerry Accettola's calling hours. Jerry was a baseball man, longtime umpire. He stocked vending machines for a living and made enough to raise a pull barn behind his house to fill it with baseball memorabilia collected over a lifetime, purportedly worth a million or more, including that of your county's most famous resident and the Panhandle Athletic Association Club's most accomplished veteran, Denton True Young; or simply, Cy. You hadn't known Jerry died, you say. You know who Willy saw in line? Sammy Nonitti, he says. Lives in Columbus now. He'd be the grandson of the Sam you knew. He is a stocky kid, Willy says, went to college. Before him, they were all railroaders, before machines did all the work. Not only that, Willy says, they'd just been down there the week before, to the R.K. Franklin funeral home, too. Bruno Opizzi had died. He was married about seventy years to Augusta, who still works as the cook at the Catholic high school. They had eleven boys before they had their girl, and came from outside of Midvale. You should've seen the line, he says. You hadn't known any of this.

"Everybody's kicking the bucket," you tell the boys.

Willy Jr. doesn't seem to be paying any attention to anything you're saying now. "You want to wash up, Uncle Jack? Your hands, I mean."

"They have you practicing, buddy?" you ask the older boy.

He nods. "Yeah, morning and afternoon."

"Why don't you tell that coach—Barr-*ett*—to go to hell?"

Willy Jr. comes over and paws your shoulder. "Come on, Uncle Jackie, let's wash up." You oblige and start pushing yourself up again. Willy Jr. sets his glasses up to his forehead and squints at your remote control a moment before shutting off your television, making old Bob Vila vanish as quick as Moon on the basement wall.

Blooming and Fading

You place the needle down on an old Tennessee Ernie Ford, get it crackling and spinning. You scoot sideways over to your chair and fall in, pulling the arm back. The feet kick up. You reach down to the side and grab hold of a liter of Leroux, sweet blackberry brandy. You haven't been much of a drinker in years and years, but somebody, somewhere, thought it a good gift for you at some time, and you've kept it under your sink in the kitchen. You steady an old tumbler on your lap and pour in a glass full. It tastes a little like cough syrup and goes down gagging at first. You're sipping slow and hear Ernie talking about weak minds and strong backs and before long he's sick and tired of being lived up like a Christmas tree, giving up on those blonde-haired women.

You got it in the back, a numbing, shooting pain traveling from just above your ass and scraping down your right leg. You're on to your second glass, drinking it now fairly fast, the Leroux smoothing out, and that sciatic nerve easing up before long. You get up to flip to the other side, leave the leg-rest kicked up, and you can't quite get the needle where it's supposed to go on the record, but it hits some place and music's coming back out, and you're clippity-cloppin' along with Ernie. Then he starts on about Philadelphia lawyers making love to Hollywood maids, that old Woody Guthrie number, Woody a warrior for all that's right and just and decent and fair, and that could make him money and get him a little applause.

You can feel the brandy warming you up, lifting you off your feet, connecting you on through the wall behind your television set to whatever else is down 2nd Street Extension, on through the South Side, over the railroad tracks that trains don't travel anymore, past the depot they've given National Historic Landmark status and turned into a visitor's attraction with a little luncheonette serving sandwiches and coffee on the inside, up Historic Center Street. Historic is right. There were more workers in that rail yard than anywhere in the world, at one time, but that was before your time even.

Ernie's got you scooting past the new library, past the elementary school, past St. Theresa's, past where the high school once burnt to the ground, past Moretti's shoe shop, past the skeletal remains of old coal tipples, past where the drive-in pictures used to show, on through the fork and the Y Tavern and the old dime jukeboxes, rolling you down the hill near the West End Restaurant, long demolished, straight on in to the sulphur-orange Stillwater Creek, moving over old rock, you coming up, your eyes squeezing tightly shut, you sopping wet from the still water. You shake your head as you sit, your eyes closed, you whipping dry like an old beagle, your own romance of the evening blooming and fading, your head a tilt-a-whirl. At one time, you'd have had about ten Camel cigarettes by now, too, one after the other, but your ashtrays haven't done anything but lie there like drunk Polacks for decades. Worthless bums.

Time for a piss.

*　*　*

Now, you're lying back, your legs all the way out and you shake off your untied boots, and Ernie's talking about going back to the house and baking pies, and you can feel the boo-gie-woogie in your hips, a little topsy-turvy in your gut. You lean your chin up on your chest and focus in on the record jacket, sitting right in front of the phonograph. It's a sketch with an orange and yellow background. Ernie's leaning his face on one hand, looking at something somewhere else. His eyes are wide open, his mustache pencil-thin, his curly hair combed back straight. Looks like some little kid has written all over the front of the jacket. This was the first record lying on the small stack, one you haven't heard in how long, dust caked on the cover.

This is where you get sucked back into your chair, from the Stillwater, from the West End, from the shoe shop, from the depot. You've come back like a boomerang and feel your ass in the chair, your legs getting numb and turning to needles and back to numb, your sciatic nerve scraping back down the side of your leg like a fillet knife. You're falling back in with nothing to grasp hold of the way down, and you feel the heavy dismay of never having gotten anywhere tonight except right here.

What are you on? Fourth glass? Fifth?

Your free hand has fallen completely asleep and you hold it down to the side, wiggling your fingers, and the blood takes longer than it ought to, to come back. The phone's ringing and you yell for it to go to hell. It stops for a while and starts up again. You tell it the same thing. The wind is moving the branches of the trees outside and you tell them to go to hell. Two of the three bulbs in your ceiling fan light fixture are out and you tell them to go to hell before spitting on the carpet next to you. The record's over with but still moving around and around and around, that needle blipping on each rotation, that skipping noise you haven't heard in years, that popping and clicking, and you tell it to go to hell, too.

Ernie Ford never dug number nine coal, no matter how many times he sang it. He wasn't born in no drizzling rain. Middle name was Jennings, somebody said, not fighting and not trouble. No fists of iron, no fists of steel, neither going to get you, ever, never at all. Ernie Ford's a first-class phony, a big bag of wind, and he can go straight to hell, too. And so can Woody Guthrie and the rest of them. The next time you spit, your body feeling its sweat and sitting in the same spot, you aim for the record jacket. You get close the first time. The rest ends up on you.

This is where you'll sleep a good while tonight, right here in this well-built, American-made La-Z-Boy recliner, and that record will keep turning whether any music's coming out or not.

Entombed

This is when everything starts coming apart.

Since Speedy got killed, you've been restless. It was that big German police dog up the road. Maimed him something awful. You still keep table scraps in the bowl outside Speedy's box, hoping the police dog takes notice, so you can get a clear shot. And then that neighbor will think it over before letting some big bastard dog of his attack another little one belonging to somebody else. You leave an old six-gun on the supper table just in case. Your eyesight's going, don't forget. If you're to shoot a damn thing, you'll need more bullets, more than however many you have, so you get yourself ready enough and head uptown to the Super Walmart. They advertise on television during *Price is Right*.

It's been months since you've driven anywhere. On your own anyway. You've never even been to a Walmart, but the drive ought to be no more than twenty minutes. Two towns over. No, shouldn't be more than twenty minutes. They say if you take the four-lane, it only takes ten if you're really moving, but you go through town, up Old 250, the business route.

There are Cash Advances and Skilled Games and Dollar Stores everywhere, up and down 250. It's late winter, and all the snow is gone. Where the West End restaurant has been paved over a long time now, there is a trailer that sells ice cream, year-round the sign says, called The Creamery;

a car wash across the street says, WASH YOUR CAR, WASH YOUR DOG. You heard excitement that a new oil company is putting its main headquarters next to the Mattress Matters, where the Reynolds Mining offices used to be. Helen says Cousin Moon's property is to be cleared and dozed so they can bust up the belly of the earth for a test well. Willy Jr. is hoping they get a lease out at his place, too. Everyone's talking big money.

* * *

The parking lot alone seems bigger than the sewer pipe had ever been, but it probably isn't. Maybe. Who knows? It is full of automobiles, that's for sure. When do any of these people work? You park in a handicapped spot, though you don't own a sticker saying you can. You step out of the cab and take a grocery cart sitting in the next space over. You lean in towards it while you walk up to the doors. They open on their own. On the inside, somebody as old as you says hello and salutes. He's wearing a blue vest, his hands full of smiley stickers.

They have everything you could imagine at Walmart. Argento's has always been a good-sized grocery, but nothing like this place, built up in the '90s sometime. Truly, a person could come here, get his eyeglasses, tomato seeds, topsoil, a funeral tie, pair of undershorts, and a jug of milk without ever leaving the store. No chance the workers are organized. Don't bet on it.

You move past magazine stands with nearly bare-titted women staring right at you, right at little kids punching their mothers' sweat-panted legs. Some of these women holler for the kids to shut the hell up. Goddamn, they're fat; everybody's fat.

You head up a long aisle and move past television game machines singing loud music. Ten-, twelve-year-old boys stand next to each other moving remote controls side-to-side and looking lively as hell, though they aren't talking, just sort of grunting, biting their lips, and looking dejected as all get-out when the other wins, or something. Good for them being so free. They'd been driving ponies in the mines a few years back. But there are grown men, too, full-sized, probably with kids of their own, standing at the machines right next to them, no sleeves on their shirts, playing games on televisions. They're fat, too—the sons, the fathers. Grown men. Kid games. Their fat wives are still back in the packaged sweets aisle, no doubt.

They have a druggist along the way, too, a whole pharmacy in the corner of the Walmart. A muscleman, what passes for being in shape, stands over there scanning a shelf at the end of one aisle. MASS BUILDER $39.99, it advertises. Somebody else, tall as can be, six-foot-five probably, fills his arms with GLUTEN-FREE FLOUR nearby. You keep moving.

Walmart has housewares of all kinds, cheap-made, metal-framed davenports and ceiling fans and electronic pianos. You go past the bicycles. At the end of those aisles are fluorescent tight shorts and helmets. Beyond those, just a few yards up, are bright orange vests and camouflage. There's a uniform for everything these days, and somebody somewhere is making a hell of a lot of money telling people they ought to dress up to ride a bike or shoot a rabbit.

And the people, nearly all of them, are talking on a telephone or fidgeting with their thumbs across little machines, looking down into their gadgets and then looking back up and looking down again, and nearly walking into one another. Fast music is playing overhead, sounding like a whole lot of nothing.

You come to the very far corner of the whole place— OUTDOORS—where they hang heavy jackets and ball caps and long underwear and overalls. You look close at the tags. *China. El Salvador. Indonesia.* Everywhere but here. Anywhere but here. Your legs are barely holding you steady and you go to a big glass case in the center of the section. Ammunition. And that's where you run into Willy Jr., arms full of fishing lures.

"What are you doing out today, Uncle Jackie, all the way up here?" Willy Jr.'s sideways smirk tilts up, but he seems more concerned than bemused, and his eyes stare at your forehead or over your shoulders or to the shelves, but not really at you.

"Nothing, buddy."

"You after something in particular?" he asks, looking into your empty cart. "You didn't take the four-lane, did you?"

"No." You should've just gone right to the bullets in the first place.

"Let me get somebody to help you, Uncle Jackie." Willy Jr. sets his lures down into your cart and walks towards a stock boy. The two go back and forth, Willy Jr. talking out the side of his mouth mostly, him leaning in and touching the young guy's shoulder. Both of them are laughing by the end.

The kid walks up, his mouth sort of hanging open like he's been to the dentist, and asks, "Is there something I can help you with today?"

"The hell's the matter with you?"

"Sorry?" The dopey kid has big hooks through his earlobes and a tattoo up his forearm. There's nothing shocking about him: he's just a dumb kid. Everybody's got tattoos now, sure, not just the carnies or zingari. You know that, but this tattoo is all writing wrapped around in a circle.

"What the hell is that?" you ask.

"Excuse me?" the kid asks.

"That, right there."

"Oh, that's a quote from *Star Wars*."

"From what?"

"It's a movie, Uncle Jackie. It's good, you ought to see it," Willy Jr. says.

"It's actually from the new one. Can I help you with something?" the kid asks again.

"No," you tell him.

"You all right, Uncle Jackie?" Willy Jr. asks.

"Never been better."

You leave the grocery cart where it is and will go out on your own legs, if you can manage. You end up bracing on whatever is in front of you to stay steady as you're able. Big metal bins of movies or something, shelves of candy bars, cases of greeting cards, whatever. Once outside, you make it to your truck. It's taking everything just to get from the front of the store to the handicapped space.

You open your truck when you get to it, everything blurring up together, and grab hold of the headrest with one hand and the door with the other. You stay like that a minute or two and then sort of fall into the cab, laying your head back, pushing in the clutch, starting her up, and finding a gear.

You head left out of the parking lot instead of the way you'd come and turn your two-ton onto the four-lane. You just want home.

Five or so minutes has gone by, that's all, maybe less, and a patrolman pulls from the side of the freeway and puts on his lights. He's in a big sedan, eight-cylinder, sure. You drive a couple, three more miles, and that cop keeps following behind. Before you come to the exit near St. Theresa's, where just about everybody you ever knew is buried, the cop puts his sirens on, too, so you pull off the exit and off the road altogether.

The cop's in his vehicle for a while before getting out. You watch in the driver's side mirror as he moves slow as hell, keeping one hand on what's probably a nine-millimeter. Looks like Mr. Salvadori, your old neighbor, just as tall, squared shoulders, right down to the crooked nose. Could be a grandson of Vic, maybe even a great-grandson Vic's been dead so long.

You roll down your window.

"Sir," the officer begins, speaking up, "your license and registration, please?"

You nod your head and feel beneath the seat.

The officer checks your card, keeps looking at the license, and says, "I know a relation of yours: Will Horvath."

"That's my brother-in-law." You look at the cop's face. Plump and smooth. He isn't fat, but his chin sinks right into his neck, like there isn't even a chin at all. "Or you probably mean my sister's son. He's your friend, huh?"

"I know him. See him at the range sometimes. I worked at United before I got on the highway patrol."

"What nationality are you?"

"Nationality?"

"Your people, where they from?"

"Me? I'm Welsh, German. And American Indian. Cherokee."

"Cherokee?"

"Yeah, my great, great-grandpa, I think it was. Something like that. Two or three greats."

You speak a little more about whatever. The cop finally says, "Mr. August, you were traveling down the wrong side of the freeway. You're liable to get yourself killed. Or somebody else." He hands you back your license.

"Fact is, I'd never taken this way before, knew it seemed funny to me."

The cop looks you over. "I'm going to have you turn around up about one-hundred yards at the end of this on-ramp. Stay on the berm as you go for now. I'll follow you home."

* * *

You hadn't told the cop very much, but you must've mentioned Helen, because she's there when you get to the house. The cop doesn't ask you anything more, but he speaks to Helen outside, resting his hand on and occasionally patting your dump truck. You knock out a couple mud dauber nests from the windowsill, go on in, and lie down on your bed. After a bit, Helen comes inside and grabs your wrist. She's shaking it and hollering: "I don't want you driving that truck anymore. It's not safe to take on the road. And your eyesight isn't what it used to be. You're going to get yourself killed. You stay put." You say nothing to her, roll to your side, and go to sleep.

* * *

It's days later and you want out of your house. You're looking but can't find your keys to the dump, so you telephone Helen. Before you can get a word in edge-wise, she starts on you, says you'll be headed to Sisters of Mercy the next day.

"The hell for?"

"It'll just be a little while, Jackie," she says, "so you can recuperate."

"Recuperate from what?"

115

She says your back and legs are just about ruined, and if you want to have any use from them again, you'll have to rest at the Retirement Community wing and hope their condition improves. She's been talking it over with Willy Jr. for some time now, she says.

The sisters established the nursing home, across from the hospital, when the dilapidated mental ward was renovated and became the county's premier *retirement community*. You've seen it enough times. A walkway attaches the two buildings, so when inside you're not too far from either wing. You've never known of anybody who's gone in and come back out. It's an old folks' home, simply put. A young person might stop awhile there to recuperate, but when you're looking down the barrel at ninety, you go and stay. They don't smash you right off, just cave you in.

Last time you saw it, Coke Haas was decked out with tubes of all kinds, in his veins, in his crotch. Coke didn't know who you were, and you never went back. You should've given Coke the same treatment you'd have given to any old rabbit dog, no longer worth a damn. Now you're supposed to go and get better. Helen says it is to only be temporary, and that it will be good to get out of the old house. To be taken care of for a little while. It will cost an arm and a leg, she says, but they'll lease your property out for gas and between the upfront money, monthly royalties, and what's in your bank account, it will take care of itself. It'll all run out, you know, and the government will kick in.

You must sleep most of the day before Willy Jr. comes over in the afternoon and boxes up your flannel shirts, a wool sweater, your shoes, house slippers, a pair of brown loafers you've only worn to weddings and then funerals, and several hats. Willy Jr. also takes undershirts, shorts, and socks. Helen has sent a pot of polenta and beef gravy for your supper tonight. Willy Jr. says they'll be back in the morning, that his mother, up in her eighties, your little sister, shouldn't have to be a caregiver for anyone but herself.

* * *

Sometime past midnight, bright outside with a Full Lenten Moon, you slump in your kitchen. You feel like you have the flu for the first time in a long time, a fire swirling in your belly wanting to come upwards and bust your head open wide.

Your kitchen table is sturdy and hasn't been moved in probably a half century. It seems smaller now but holds you up. You and Papa built it for Mama in 1932 when you were nine, two years before they got him in the Rosemarie. On the table are scattered newspaper ads from the past week's editions of *The Daily Recorder*. The pot of polenta has barely been touched, and your revolver lies sideways across the Sports section. Two golden-necked bullets sit beside the empty chamber, one erect, the other flat. Another is somewhere under one of the ads.

You never did get that police dog. And you'll never shoot into yourself either, you know, but wish somebody else would.

Your eyes feel like they're sinking deep, backwards into your skull. You focus on the six-gun, .45 caliber, single-action. It was given to you by Papa probably not long after you two built that table. You take the upright bullet and hold it firmly between your thumb and forefinger. You lean your head forward, rest it on your right hand, and feel the cold of the straight-walled cartridge dig into the stubble of your cheek, as your elbow pushes into the American chestnut tabletop. You press the bullet in deeper, so hard that it's liable to go right through your face. Your chest and legs feel small, all your weight settling in your gut. You're an old man, brittle-boned, end of the line.

This is what it's come to.

* * *

You look at the kitchen clock on the wall. Morning is coming, like it or not, and you'll go from home, the home Papa built new in America with Zio Federico, the home Mama lived in until she went for good, too, like everybody else that came over here.

Below the clock sits the ceramic plate, secured to the wall, that you put up years ago for Mama. There are two, the other belonging to Helen. On the plate is a drawing of Val di Non. Some relation sent it over long after Papa was gone, probably the middle of the century. The mountains are yellow and green and the big man-made lake, the lake of Saint Justina, the virgin martyr, sits in the middle, damming up the Noce River.

Papa, by his mid-thirties, had come over several times, shipped out of Genoa. Each time, he saw new corners of the big country he hadn't known existed before, and even had a first wife somewhere else. Your papa found no gold up in Alaska, lost the wife somewhere along the way—she ran off, somebody said—but he did find a pickaxe and coal here in Ohio, clay beneath that. After his final trip, he sent for Mama, half his age. Then his brother returned, too. And this became home for good. You never saw Val di Non firsthand, but heard it was something. Cousin Moon was born there, of course, and then saw it again, as a young man, when he fought the War, and again when he went back and worked on that dam. Said that plate didn't do it justice.

You never made it anywhere farther than Cleveland.

You move the bullet from your face and grip it in your fist, taking the revolver in your free hand, both elbows posted now. Your insides twist up tight as a coil spring as you flip open the chamber, place both bullets, and move the papers off to find the third. With the gun half-full, you close it. The table stays put as you lift yourself up. With your left hand, you grab the back of a kitchen stool to steady yourself.

Now, you point the gun outwards and cock the hammer. You have to sort of turn it sideways so you can push the trigger in. You're liable to kill yourself this way. You aim it well enough and shoot right through Val di Non. A piece of ceramic blows back, bounces off something, and cuts your left cheek, deep enough that it doesn't bleed much immediately. The rest of the plate goes everywhere. Blood starts to trickle down and off your chin. Your legs feel like themselves all of a sudden. In this moment, you could probably duckwalk the low mines of Ohio's foothills. You tug on the hammer again, pull so hard you nearly break your thumb, and turn it towards your supper table. You end up firing two more shots. One goes through the chestnut and the other blows your sister's pot to the ground. Still bracing your body with your left arm on the back of the chair, you lay the gun down, emptied out.

You move from the kitchen and walk sideways as both your hands press on the chairs to keep you from falling. You don't look to see if there is any of the plate left, on the wall or at the table beside you. Your hands clench at nothing but the flatness of the walls, leaning yourself into them to stay balanced, sliding as you go. You walk around the corner, past Mama's old room and to your own. Without taking off your boots or pants, you tumble onto your mattress and go to sleep in your own home for the last time, your face bleeding into your pillowcase and drying you to it.

*   *   *

In the morning, neither Helen nor Willy Jr. mentions the gun, the splintered table, or the beef gravy spilled across the linoleum.

HOLY COMMUNION

Holy Communion

You fully remove the acrylic comforter from your face after being awakened by Carl walking brisk circles around the cramped room, his morning exercises.

"Got to stay in top condition," Carl says, "keep my weight down."

"They've got some big ones here." You spread your hands wide and adjust in your wheelchair.

"What?" Carl asks.

"Fat people. The help is fat. Seems to me they used to be a hell of a lot leaner couple years ago."

Carl takes off his ball cap and forms both hands into a cone around his ear, leaning towards you, his roommate, from the other side of the ten-by-twelve lodging the two of you have been allotted for your combined nine-thousand-dollar-a-month room and board fee.

"Now, couple hundred pounds or more, each."

"A hundred and fourteen out of a hundred and fourteen," Carl boasts.

"The hell you talking about?" You take off your glasses and push up from either side of the chair. You fall forward on the very slim and uneven mattress.

"One-hundred and fourteen. Every one of them. Every clay plate shot up, I shot it down." Carl pumps one fist and with the other hand points towards the row of dusty trophies aligned on the couple feet of shelf above his bed. Each of you has your own shelf. Carl's has a Bronze Star, too. Yours is empty, except for just a few photos and trinkets, including a picture from Europe of Mama that Helen has placed up there. She's staring straight-faced, an aged teenager by then. Either Carl has no family left, or they just never come by.

Carl had been several years behind you at St. Theresa's and may have even graduated high school. You met again, years later, at the sewer pipe and you can only recollect that Carl had a gained a reputation as an excellent bricklayer, working out of Local 6. At one time, he could've worked most anywhere. The sewer pipe always kept several bricklayers from the local, along with hundreds of clay workers. Carl's steady hands and sharp eye maintained the kilns, beehives, and you must've tended him more than once, though you can't quite remember. If you wanted work after the mines shut down and the railroad quit running, the sewer pipe was about it.

As far as you can tell, Carl had saved his money. He would sit in the back of Argento's in the old days, after hours, but only to watch the men play cards. Carl was never a drunk like so many of the beat-up old clay workers who'd tended him. How many men did you go get from their homes, early morning, and get them to work, sobered up just enough so they wouldn't lose their jobs? Carl enjoys a glass of beer one day and wine the next at Mercy, that's it. Nowadays, though, his long, calloused mitts shake like they're vibrating and he'll spill any drink you give him.

This was about all you knew of Carl prior to your living arrangement. Now, you find your life winding down and shared with what was once an athletic, quick-witted half-German, half-Polack who fiddles with Rubik's Cubes and a mouth organ, time to time.

"When's that priest supposed to be here, Carl?"

"Oh, I suppose so," Carl says.

"Damn it, Carl, when's that priest coming? It is Sunday, isn't it?" You're hollering loud, the way Willy Jr. hollers at you.

"Oh, I think he should've been here by now." Father Ralph Nowak, who visits the patients at Mercy every Sunday, even the handful of non-Catholics, will be on his way this afternoon following his own Masses.

You glance at the digital clock, a gift from Willy Jr.'s family that previous Christmas which is positioned by your bed next to a 13-inch flat panel television, the alarm never set. 8:23 AM, it flashes.

"You want a muffin? They got muffins, I think. Blueberry ones, probably," Carl says, still moving.

"Sure." While working, you never took sweets. You might take a couple bananas, one in your hip pocket and one in your hand when you'd leave home in the morning. You could eat them quickly and toss the peels.

"How about some coffee, too? They got that good coffee down there. Cream? Sugar?"

"That'd be all right."

Carl takes off. You expect him back in about an hour or so with nothing, after Carl makes all of his morning rounds. You pull the comforter over your face, legs hanging off the side of the bed, slippers still on, and drift in and out of bad sleep.

* * *

It is probably around nine o'clock when Carl comes back. "Hey, ol' friend, you want a muffin? Maybe some coffee?" Carl had been sharp at one time; before he was thrown in here, he must've been. But, sharp or not, he is happy. "Be back in no time, ol' friend," Carl says.

This second time around takes no time, and Carl has a muffin and coffee, black, half-spilled out, just in time for Renee to take you two to breakfast.

"Oh, I see Carl has something for you. Carl, honey, why don't you set that aside," Renee, the biggest, but sweetest aide says. She takes the muffins and coffee from his hands and places them on the end table. "We'll head down to breakfast in a minute. Carl, have you cleaned up for today?"

"The problem at my age," Carl says, removing his hat and wiping his chin, "is I got less hair to comb but more face to wash." He leaves.

Renee approaches and you turn away in your bed. "That's all right," you say. Your legs, once tree trunks placed below a slim waist and narrow hips, like a big league catcher's, now look more like those of Speedy after his run-in with the police dog.

"Let's go, Jack. Eggs and toast is waiting." Renee pulls the covers off and coaxes you to sit up. The way Renee smiles makes her brown face and neck round and bright like the moon.

"That's all right, sweetheart, you can have it."

"Come now, Jack. What would that sister of yours say to me if she was to know you weren't eating any breakfast?"

You straighten up with a little prodding and, with her hoisting, scoot into the waiting wheelchair.

*   *   *

Halfway down, you pass the communal room where a whole bunch of worn-out faces focus on whatever in all directions. A group who still have their heads but nothing much else play 500 Rum, and the television is set to *The 700 Club*, even at a Catholic hospital. You speak up as you tell no one in particular that Pat Robertson is a no-good, two-faced bastard snake. You point with your right index finger at all that decrepitude and say, "They ought to throw 'em all in a gully and doze the damn thing over."

"Jack, that's terrible," Renee says, but doesn't pick up any pace.

You fold your hands on your lap while she stops to push the brakes on the wheels farther from the rubber of the tire so that it won't catch.

When she does it, you see Renee's little diamond and ask, "Who you married to?"

"Now, Jack, I told you I will be married in two months."

"St. Theresa's?"

"No, just a small ceremony. We were each married before, remember."

"Caruso." You roll your *R*.

"That's right."

"How is your father-in-law, Fred, anyway? Still welding pipe?"

"Oh, Fred's been retired at least ten years now."

"Is that right?" It is something: Freddy Caruso, the baby of that family, now retired.

"How about the boy, the one you're going with?"

"Was laid off, but just got on with the oil and gas."

You arrive at the dining area. It smells like a school cafeteria and looks like one, too, with just as many nuns, though these ones are a hell of a lot older than those from your youth, some of them locked up here like you.

"Here, Jack, sit next to Carl." Renee wheels you next to your roommate across from the Toth sisters, twins and pretty, at one time anyway. Juanita is deaf and Ellen just about dead following a third stroke. Runny eggs and soggy bacon are placed in front of you.

"What do you say, ol' friend?" Carl is rubbing his sleeves up and down. "Rub, Jack, rub," Carl says. "It warms it up. Makes it hot." Carl works the nylon sleeves at some pace. "Truck drivers wear this material to stay warm, I suppose. They break down, they can rub the night away." His hands go fast and his teeth bite down hard, lips pulling back like a coondog baring its teeth at the base of a tree.

Renee brings hot oats over. "If you don't like the eggs, have some oatmeal, Jack," she says and places the spoon in your hand.

"No thanks. None for me."

"It's sweet." She goes to talk with some of the other help by a makeshift fruit bar.

"To hell with it," you say and toss the spoon back towards the table. It misses and falls onto the floor. You move your arms back and lay your hands on top of your knees.

Carl's eyes, which are barely visible through the wrinkled slits on his face, focus deeply on the Henry's Asphalt patch at the breast of his jacket. He says, "I wonder how they engineer a material like this." Carl moves his hands to his belly now. "Why don't you give a rub? Feel that warmth. Piping, piping, piping hot."

Maria Monticelli, which all the help pronounces like it has an *S* in it, comes up from behind and leans on the chair next to you. She wears an ankle-length, paisley housedress, the pattern looking like a million teardrops. "Hey there fella, hey there fella, you want to come with me?" Maria's voice clangs as fast as her chicken legs shake. There was a time, decades ago, that she was the star majorette.

You try a piece of bacon and chew it like bubblegum.

"Hey now, fella, you wouldn't believe the things you hear around this place," Maria says. "I asked you nicely, now I'll ask again, are you coming with me or not?"

You point at Carl. "The weasel, take him." Really, Carl looks like a ferret more than a weasel, the kind you used to keep in each pocket of a short coat while rabbit-hunting years back.

Carl looks towards Maria, says, "What?" and bumps pink lemonade down onto his pant legs.

"You coming along ol' boy or what?" She shakes like an old engine finally turned over and with just enough juice to go any which way.

Carl takes off his ball cap and forms both hands into a cone around his ear again.

"You boys sicken me, nearly a hundred and nothing to show for it." Maria turns away.

"Oh, like I told him, hundred-fourteen out of a hundred-fourteen. Perfect." Carl smiles and winks at you. What that wink means, who knows?

Maria goes off some other way and Carl rambles at length about a whole lot of things, about the alligator that ate his dog in Florida, about tracking a moose miles and miles into Canada, about his uncle having met the Kaiser back in Europe.

Renee comes back before too long. "Jack, you didn't touch a thing." She pulls you from the table and says, "Come on, Carl."

While Renee wheels you from your meal, you move your feet on the ground as fast as the chair. There are art prints framed and hanging in the hallway by someone named Robert Duncan. One has cows at a fence in winter as a small boy passes by; it is called "Curious Onlookers," according to a little metal piece at the base. Another, called "Swept Away," has a young girl sitting out on her stoop, reading a book. They hung up "Curious Onlookers" and "Swept Away" at an old folks' home. Nobody would believe you if you told them.

You have a hard time bringing yourself to look into most of the doorways on the way. Inside are those you knew and those you don't, but at this place, it doesn't make much difference, regardless of what they dug, what language their fathers spoke, and what kind of suppers their mothers had fixed. You notice that Coke Haas is missing from the room in which he is usually tangled up with all those tubes. "Where's Coke?" you ask.

"Oh, they took him to Intensive Care last night. That flu took just about everything out of Mr. Haas."

You lean forward and turn your head back towards Coke's room. "Should've buried the bastard ten or twenty years ago. A low-grade bum."

"Jack, you don't mean that."

"The hell I don't."

"Do you need to use the restroom, Jack?" Renee asks as she wheels you in, setting the chair next to your bed.

"No, I'm fine."

"You know Roger doesn't mind helping you."

Taking a shit is the worst part of the day. You can't angle the chair enough to make it to the toilet without some assistance. At nighttime, you don't bother even getting up anymore. The first time you had pissed your bed, months back, you never mentioned it to Renee and she never said a word about it while she changed the sheets the next morning. You appreciated her kindness. Now, you have a hard time even wiping yourself after using the commode and whoever helps you is generally matter-of-fact about the whole thing, the fact being you can't even wipe your own ass anymore.

You take a few moments before saying, "That'd be all right."

She asks, "What happened to Carl?"

Across the hall, you both hear him. "I'm eighty-seven years old. Probably the oldest person here. I'll bet anything."

She goes over.

"Oh hi, Star," he says, coming back in. "I think George is sick. Somebody better check on him. I worked for the same company for eighty years, believe it or not." He sits down and looks at you, saying, "I'm ninety-four years old. Believe that?"

She leaves them and Carl starts on about Give 'Em Hell Harry, maybe the best president this country has ever seen, didn't take shit from anyone.

* * *

It isn't long before Roger comes into the room. "What do you say, Jack?"

You sit upright.

"Renee said you needed to use the john." Roger's tattooed arms rest on his hips. He is short and blocky.

"Nearly every day, my whole damn life." Roger is pretty light in the loafers. He's a part-time bartender at Tiny's Tavern and takes old coal miners to shit on Tuesdays, Thursdays, and Sundays for minimum wage each week.

"Well then," Roger says, grabbing the wheelchair's handles. He greets Carl, too. "How you doing today, Captain?"

Carl smiles and says, "Shazam, I believe."

He shuts the bathroom door behind you. "All right now, Jack, unbuckle your belt for me."

It takes you a minute.

"Okay, let's stand you up so that we can take down your pants."

"I can do it. I tell you every goddamn time, leave me alone. Just leave me alone."

But you can't. You lean your body on Roger's shoulder.

"All right now, Jack," Roger says, "sit down on the toilet and I'll be back when you need me."

You had held it in the day before when Roger was off. Last evening, though, you'd eaten a chipped beef and white gravy over biscuits supper. It did a number on your stomach. It takes everything to start to piss and it hurts. You wish Mercy had those bathroom exhaust fans that hum loudly, like in people's homes these days, some kind of privacy. You're a long way from the miserable old outhouse, sat up behind the home when you were a kid, but at least no one bothered you there. You focus on the wall, studying the mortar between the blocks where the hot water pipe comes out and think it's really something that a queer bartender is about to wipe your ass and Fred Caruso's boy is a marrying a heavyset black woman. It's a mixed-up world, and people just better get used to it.

You eventually finish everything up but wait several minutes, your pants down around your ankles, your head bowed.

"All right," you finally call.

Roger comes in, props you up against his shoulder again, and says, "Let's clean you up."

"I got it," you say as you lean on Roger.

"You sure, Jack?"

You nod and wipe yourself mostly clean. Roger finishes what's left and helps pull your pants back up and buckles your belt for you. He sets you back into the chair and wheels you out. As you return to the far corner of the room where you will have a chance to wash your hands, Carl is already mid-sentence, "Unless it was Dean Martin; he's from over in Steubenville, you know. Could have been him, too. I'll ask the priest."

"Remember," Roger says, "you have PT in a little while, Jack."

"PT's for the weasel, not for me. I failed the physical," you say.

"Sorry?"

"My right drum," you say, tugging at your oversized ear, "it's been broken since '34, when I was eleven. He's the vet. A gunner in the Battle of the Bulge. They didn't take me on account of my hearing."

Roger is now holding the remote control for Carl's bed and shaking it.

"Carl calls it PT because that's what they call it in the Army Air Force," you say.

"Oh, well what do you call it?"

"Bullshit."

"Ha!"

*　*　*

An hour or so later, Roger pushes you into the large open area filled with doctors' tables and young women you had been told were physical therapists and aides to physical therapists. This particular wing of Mercy smells of plastic. The rest of the place smells like a possum whose head had been smashed days ago by a full-sized pickup. Roger hoists you onto the table, and the bare white of your lower limbs, covered with green veins and loose flesh, partly shows as your corduroy pant legs pull up. The bone underneath looks crooked and busted, like someone has taken a sledge and hammered a lightning rod every which way.

133

A plain blonde, whose name you have never cared to learn, approaches. "How've you been feeling?"

"Oh, better and better all the time, baby."

"Good. Just sit still on the table." The blonde woman never looks up from her chart and you haven't moved. She has all the personality and looks of a clean chunk of number six coal.

"How come you never wear makeup?" you ask.

"Can you lift your legs for me at all?" she asks.

You lift them just a bit and set them down.

"Okay," she continues, "you're going to need to hold them just a little longer." This all happens several times a week.

You don't move.

"I said I need you to lift your legs back up."

You stare at Roger and ask, "Blondie say something?"

"Behave, Jack," he says.

Finally, you raise both your legs as best you can, hold them for a bit, maybe four seconds, and set them down.

"Up again," the therapist coaxes you.

When the blonde bends down, a fair amount of cleavage spills forth for such a thin woman. "What do you think of that, buddy?" you ask Roger.

Roger, queer or not, doesn't respond, his arms crossed now.

"That's what I thought," you say.

"We're going to have you turn on your side. Can you do that for me?" This woman hasn't smiled once and makes no direct eye contact with anyone.

"Nope."

"Let me help," Roger says.

"Nope, I'm done. Meet me in the back of my two-ton, blondie."

The therapist says, "The sooner you cooperate, the sooner we'll be done. Now, if you would, turn onto your side, please."

Roger moves in and sets you to each side, first the right and then the left. While on either side, you put your arms out and move them up and down and start clicking your tongue against the roof of your mouth.

"Fine. I suppose this can be all for today," she says, looking up. "Remember, you're paying good money to be here. You should make the most of the services you're offered."

"Well, let me tell you, honey, I don't expect to be here a whole hell of a lot longer. Once I get my legs back, I'm going home." Maybe Helen will come get you. Maybe you'll even get to take Willy Jr.'s boys rabbit hunting with that new dog they're supposed to have. Maybe not, too. You sleep most of the daytime usually, but when you lie awake at night, you are sure you'll make it home eventually. Why get up in the morning otherwise?

The therapist pats your legs and walks away, bending her head back towards her chart.

* * *

Carl says almost nothing to or in front of Father Ralph Nowak on Sunday afternoons. He just nods and stares while the priest reads a little scripture, gives the Eucharist.

You are back in your chair, the blanket pulled up to your chin.

Father Ralph is a tall, pot-bellied man, broad-shouldered and even wider at the hips. He had once told you that his father was an autoworker in Toledo for thirty-seven years and dropped over dead one week into retirement. You remember that story, not because it was told to you several times over, the priest trying to explain your fortune of nine decades of life, but rather because Father Ralph drives a Toyota. You'd think we lost the War. Too bad Cousin Moon weren't around still; he'd have something to say to that priest.

Father approaches you. "And how has your roommate been, Carl?"

You keep your eyes shut.

"Jack, how are you?" Father asks as he leans in.

"Top shape," you say, eyes shut still. "Brought some bread today, did you, Nowak? Do me a favor next time and bring some pierogies instead."

"Holy Eucharist, that's what it is. You ought to know that. Jack, I thought maybe you'd like to join Carl and I in a bit of reflection this afternoon." Father moves his hand towards yours.

You curl your hand into a fist so that Father Ralph can neither hold nor shake it. You open your eyes now, but peer outside, where three or four inches of snow has fallen. You remember driving the county's big dump, a green GM. After you quit the coal and clay, and after six or seven years at the sewer pipe, you spent close to a decade—off and on, part-time—on the county's road and bridge department. In the wintertime, back when you could count on real snow, terrible blizzards, you'd drive and dump ash and salt along the roadways. When you worked on the county, there were at least seventy other men there at any given time. You've heard the county is down to eighteen or nineteen now, and they're touted in the paper and recognized by the state of Ohio for efficiency. Is that what passes for progress?

"How about I just leave you with this?" the priest asks. He places a Catechism on your nightstand next to a copy of the Mercy Retirement Community Newsletter, unread, full of coupons—for what?—and gathering dust. You haven't ever read a book except one, none other that you can remember anyway. It was called *My Name is Aram* by an Armenian, which, you know, is something like a Syrian. It was just a few years ago after the local library placed boxes all over town with free books. You'd looked through and found that, a bunch of little stories with drawings. You skimmed it through, anyway. There was probably as much truth in that little book as in anything Ralph Nowak has to offer you.

"Just give it a once-over sometime." The priest taps the book with his fingers.

"Oh hell, I won't be able to get enough of it."

"Jack, Jesus always has time for anyone interested in opening up their hearts to him." The priest begins to walk away, as Carl sits smiling, closed-mouth, with his own Catechism in his lap, unopened.

"Let me ask you something: you say he has time? Time for what, I wonder?" you ask.

"Time for you, Jack. Time for anyone interested in turning their lives over to him."

"For what? Give lives for what? What the hell does he give back?" Your cover has fallen to your lap, and you retrieve your glasses from the nightstand and put them on.

"An opportunity, Jack. An opportunity to live in paradise. Eternal. At the feet of the Lord. Eternal worship."

"Sounds just delightful. And what about if I don't give it to him? What do you say happens if I stay as I am and have been? What then?"

"Jack, I think you know." The priest's words stretch out and his cheeks redden. "I don't have to tell you."

"Tell me, goddamnit."

"Hell, Jack. Hell. Forever suffering. You know that. I know you were brought up in the Church."

"Could I wipe my own ass?" you ask.

The priest sounds like he has gravel in his jowls as he presses his square jaw towards your face, saying, "Jack, you've got an opportunity, an amazing opportunity to join"—he calms himself. "Jack, this, this place, it isn't the end."

"To hell with you. And to hell with anybody who thinks he can die and come back to save anybody else. I want to tell you something: I never had to save no souls and Jesus Christ never had to dig coal. You ask me, he and I are square." You take off your glasses and place them back on the nightstand.

Carl remains smiling, hands folded.

The priest grabs his coat, hat, gloves, and scarf. He doesn't look at you as he says, "Jack, I feel sorry for you. Your body may be broken, but your mind is whole. And now, now you've let your spirit decay. The Lord has no place"—

"Good. Good, goddamnit. Let the weasel have it. He can have my place. What do you say, buddy, want my place with Jesus Christ? Wouldn't that be nice?"

Carl doesn't move.

"What the hell do you do for a living, anyway?" you say. "You ought to find some honest work."

"I have to leave. I'll see you next Sunday, Carl." Father Ralph exits and travels down the hallway. You hope he passes Maria Monticelli's room, so that she might proposition the fifty-something padre of considerable height.

Carl sits still, the only time of the week he ever remains still, usually lasting for close to an hour, at least forty-five minutes, before something breaks his concentration.

You pick at one thumbnail with the other.

Carl stands up, places the Catechism next to his First Place Piedmont Bass Competition golden trophy, and starts mumbling.

"The hell you yammering about?"

Carl mumbles out again and eventually gets out, "You might be right, I suppose," and then, "About Jesus Christ. And Father and Heaven and life and death, I guess."

"Hell, I just planted a seed and got him going. That was all. You just plant a seed. Goddamn dummy."

"Do you believe in any of it?"

"No," you say. "No, to hell with it. Just keeps guys like that fat boy in business. That's all."

"What?" Carl asks.

"Keeps 'em in business. Guys like the priest," you say louder.

Carl removes his ball cap and cups both hands to his right ear.

"Nothing. Nobody knows nothing. And it they tell you they do, a dollar to a doughnut, they're full of shit."

"Oh, probably right." Carl puts his cap back on and continues, "When I was a kid, I had trouble believing in any of it. One thing I do know, though, at the time anyway, is my mother survived."

"What?"

"My mother was widowed at thirty. Five of us to raise. Dad got cheated out of a whole lot of life, like your father, and Mom had only two or three things keeping her going. Kids and Jesus Christ. The Holy Mother, too. Hell, any kind of god wouldn't have thrown her out like that."

"Damn straight."

"But I went to church, every day. Mass, every Sunday. When I was a kid, I went. Learned Latin, served into my teens. And when Mom couldn't go on her own anymore, I drove her. She died years ago now. Ten, maybe." Carl stops, takes off his cap again, scratches his head, and says, "No, wait, probably twenty or thirty. Quite a while anyway. When I got married the last time is when I started with the Methodists. Then, after Thelma died, I become a born-again mackerel snapper." Carl snaps his fingers and giggles, a sort of blubbery, spit-filled laugh.

"I drove my mother, too. My dad never went, not that I can recall."

"You remember when you was a kid, your First Holy Communion?" Carl asks.

"No, can't say I do."

"Oh, I remember mine like it was yesterday. I was so damn nervous, kept my hands pressed together so tight, hoping all my sins had been washed away. My hands, sweating like hell between them. All I could think was I didn't want the host to touch my teeth, figured God would burn me alive right there, right in front of my own mother, and then she'd lose another one to fire." Carl stands from his bed. "Those priests meant business, you know. I remember when some of the men would want to stand in the back of St. Theresa's and Father Harrington would stop and tell 'em there were plenty of seats up front."

"They didn't move, he'd come down off that altar, boy, his robe flaring out," you say and move your arms out like a turkey flapping its wings up and down.

"Nobody, I mean nobody stood up to Father Harrington."

"He'd been a fighter, remember. Don't know how he ever let anyone in on that. Those ears of his was all mangled up something terrible," you say.

"Cauliflower," Carl says.

"And his hands were as big as gloves."

"You ever remember a priest outside of the church dressed in anything but his collar and the full getup?"

"Christ, they wear blue jeans nowadays," you say.

"Well, time marches on." Carl gathers his mouth organ and leaves down the hallway, saying something about Lawrence Welk coming on.

You pull the covers up over your face and sleep a while sitting up.

* * *

At about four-thirty, Renee enters the room with Carl close behind. She asks, "You ready to eat, Jack?"

You hear a swooshing and drop the covers so you can see.

Carl's palms rub his jacket. "Heats me up, Star," he says, smiling right at Renee.

She wheels you to supper.

Roger, the Nurse

It's Thursday, so you can expect Roger anytime now, usually comes in between breakfast and dinner. He's the beady-eyed male nurse Mercy must've hired because they'd run out of female ones. Not an official *nurse*, though, he tells you. Tattoos up and down his arms like long sleeves. And one on his neck to boot. He'll be in soon, no doubt, and ask something like, "How you feeling today, Champ?" or "How's Jack today?"

As a rule, Roger can't shut up about Brutus, his dog. Keeps the goddamn thing in his house. And the other day, you were trying to get some sleep, and he was bragging to one of the other help that Brutus prefers to sleep at the foot of his bed and lick his face in the morning. Speedy was a damn good dog, but if he'd licked your face after licking his ass, Speedy would've found out how things were. One of Roger's tattoos—the only one you can really make out—is a portrait of the damn thing. The eyes are red—who knows why—probably the pecker, too.

* * *

Watch, here he comes. Takes your towel and says, "Just one for me today, Jack?"

Like you need more than one bath towel a day.

You don't have too much in common, but he tries his best and says, "Heard your sister mention about one of your grandsons getting a good hunting dog."

"My nephews, you mean, great-nephews. I guess so, yes."

"Heard her say it looks a lot like some dog you had when you were kids," he says, shuffling around.

"Peaches. That was that old beat-up cur dog. Peaches was given to us by Mr. Salvadori. The mother had a big litter, if I remember correctly. Papa didn't want us to keep her, but I told Papa that I'd take her hunting, and I did. Bred for 'coon and squirrel, but Peaches was mixed up, would go after everything. Groundhog, possum—whatever you could pour gravy on."

"Good dog, huh?" he says and sweeps up the floor with a broom and dustpan.

"Ended up with a whole litter of pups herself. At that time, Mama and Papa hadn't been over in this country long at all and I was still awful small back then. Me and Papa were to go fish at Stillwater." You put your hands on your belly and say, "I could feel my stomach pulling in on itself just above my hips. I watched Papa throw them all in that wicker basket, one he found some place or other, loaded all them little ones. When we got to the creek, Papa said nothing while he dropped all them pups into the water. Each one of them. I don't think they could even open their eyes. After, me and Papa walked to the other side and caught spotted bass. We had a good day and plenty to eat that night."

"Well," Roger says, "lot of tough choices to make in those days, I imagine." He is holding his broom with both hands.

"We barely fed ourselves, let alone any dog. Nope, we never had many scraps to throw to old Peaches. I found her shriveled up, stomach sunk in like mine, and buried her on my own. About a year or two after is when Papa died on account of the Rosemarie explosion."

"You and your father hunted and fished a lot together?"

"Well, the bass were spawning on account of it being springtime. Papa never would've had patience otherwise. And he never hunted too much either, just me really. Always have. Cousin Moon, too. But last two or three years, I don't think I hunted once. Not squirrel, not rabbit, nothing. Since I came here, I can't remember ever going hunting."

"What'd you hunt mostly?" he asks, tilting that pan towards the basket by your bed.

"Me? I'd shoot most anything. If I had one wish, I got to tell you, it'd be to have a hunting dog here. A good dog. One for rabbit, squirrel, groundhog, and so forth. A good pointer, for ring-neck pheasant. Bet I'd get my legs to full-strength then."

"I'd actually been looking into a program where we'd have some canines come in here to keep you company. I don't think they're going for it, though," Roger says.

"I suppose I could throw one in the bathroom, keep the door shut, and take him out when no one's looking," you say, but then again, the bathroom is shared with the black guy next door. And he's already in a fix because you were pissing like a racehorse, missed the commode, and it rolled right under his door. Problem with tile floors. Otherwise, you'd find yourself one like Speedy. It could sleep at the foot of your bed. You could ask Roger for tips on how to make it comfortable; you could lick each other clean.

You tell Roger, "My hunting days are behind me anyway. Willy Jr., that's my nephew, you know. He can spend compensation checks on mounting bucks, and I'm laid up like a cripple. The way of the world."

* * *

Roger sits down on your mattress, next to your chair. If he'd stop shaving his head, you've noticed, Roger'd have all red hair. Well, at least what would be left of it: a horseshoe. His half-beard's red. He's mostly a mutt. His mother's Slovak and other things, too. You know this, about his mixed-up mother.

You get a close look and see an orange and green flag flying on his arm. Money he saves on shampoo's been invested in ink. "What the hell is that?" you ask.

"Oh," he says, "I had SANDRA written there. We split and so I figured I'd get something that'd make a little more sense." He points towards his red whiskers, thinks he's Irish because he's got red hair. Roger's probably as Irish as you. And Sandra? Roger had a woman? Don't bet on it.

Now, he starts yammering on about his old man getting second place in the wine-making contest at the American Italian Festival. Sign of the times. His old man's the same one that helped Jerry Accettola get the Panhandle Athletic Club some kind of historical status. You remember, that's the ballpark where they say Cy Young played and Babe Ruth came and watched a game. Talking baseball is about the only thing to keep Roger from talking about Brutus, who, he tells you, is like a son to him. A *son*. One thing neither of you ever had.

"Cy Young was from Peoli," you tell him. That's not too far from here, and he played at that ballpark, too, but that was before you were a kid. You tell Roger, "I remember all those Italians talking Cy Young-this and Cy Young-that, like they'd all been close personal friends." The Italiani played baseball. Guys from New York like DiMaggio and Rizzuto made it big, and most of those old loudmouths from Grant Street played, too, hoping they'd be the next Joltin' Joe.

Roger is saying he and his old man would go watch the Class A games there all the time. Tells you, "Pop used to take me around to all the ballparks. Down in the valley, up to Canton, even over to Pittsburgh to watch the Pirates at the old Three Rivers. You know it's gone now? Ever spend any time on the diamond, Jack?"

You tell him, "Sure, sure. My pop used to take me to all the parks, too. Sure he did, buddy."

Roger must know you're full of it but says anyway, "Big old legs like yours, you could've been a regular Rocky Colavito."

"My legs come from Mama's people," you tell him. "She wasn't short, for a woman anyway, probably an inch or two taller than Papa, and had big thighs." You grab your own legs when you say it. "I ended up five-ten, five-eleven until the last couple years."

While you're talking, Roger stands up and looks to the shelf above your bed where Helen has put that old family photograph of all of you.

You say, "Her hair was as black as the coal Papa dug. My eyes've always been light like hers, too, like Helen's. Helen's hair's lighter than mine or Mama's, auburn almost. And Papa, he was short, like a Sicilian or a Calabrian, and had dark circles around his black eyes, like he should've been living on Grant Street."

* * *

Roger sits back down. He's looking out the window. You don't say anything for a little bit, him running one of his hands over the fingers on the other.

He has a sorrowful look on his face today, so you finally ask what the hell's the matter.

Tells you he found out, just two days ago, that Brutus has cancer. Veterinarian says he has a fifty-fifty chance of even making it to the end of the year. Took old Brutus to the doctor's office. Kids starving everywhere you look, even in this country, even today, and he takes Brutus to get doctored. Here's the kicker: tells you with chemotherapy maybe Brutus'll make it.

You figure what's left of your hearing must finally be going with the rest of it, but nope. You heard right. With chemotherapy, he might make it to the new year.

Jesus Christ.

Hell, you've had dogs, more dogs than he is years old probably. Never any that were given chemotherapy, but dogs just the same. With what he'll be paying for treatment, you could buy a lot of dogs. So, you tell him so.

Roger says you don't understand. Says he and his friend, Travis, rescued Brutus.

"What the hell kind of name is Travis?" you ask.

Anybody asks you, Roger ought to give Brutus a taste of the shovel instead, like Papa used to do to them old tomcats hanging around the stoop. You'd prescribe shovel-therapy for Brutus if you had your medical credentials. Difference between you and Roger is he never hit coal with a pickaxe. Of course, you don't suppose you would either if you were him. Why would anyone if he didn't have to?

Roger stands up and says he'll be back later on this afternoon, says it was nice talking to you.

"Speedy was a good dog," you call to him as he goes.

He turns around, says, "That was your last beagle, right?" and leans his hand on the doorway.

"Hell yes, got Speedy a few years after Ugly died. Runny nose and a crooked eye, different color from the other, but fast as hell, probably the fastest dog I ever owned, even faster than Ugly. Found the little bugger near the old Plum Run farm, out off of Old 21. That's close to where my brother-in-law, Helen's husband's people come from. Even towards the end, Speedy's old legs'd motor and shake and get going.

Chased every rabbit in the valley, I bet. Used to be, there was a lot less rabbits around. Speedy was fortunate to have so many to get after."

Roger smiles from the door.

"We made friends quick, me and Speedy. Took him out that day when he was ready and fired my rifle right alongside him. Didn't budge. Not an inch. That's how you know you got a good one, if they keep still when you fire." You point right at Roger when you say this: "If they run scared, I can tell you right now where the next bullet ought to go. Never had that problem with Speedy, though he never did hunt really. In the old days, I'd take whatever dog I had, put him on a leash, and have Willy Jr. hide a rabbit, a dead one, out far off behind the house. Then I'd take the mutt and let him find it, see if my dog was worth a damn."

"Speedy sounds like he was a good dog, Jack."

"Put up reinforcements for that box of his, damn near falling apart. I built it back sometime before the Golden Rod mine exploded, but that little shit made a good home of it. Matter of fact, and this is the truth"—you start to laugh out loud now—"Speedy started raising tomatoes right behind that little red plywood fort."

"Tomatoes?"

"Believe it. Helen'd take scraps from the supper she'd fix for me and throw them to Speedy. Must've watched me plant beans, lettuce, cabbage, tomatoes, cut the rhubarb. Hell, I don't know how many tons of manure I ended up spreading over the years."

Really, you should've been buried alive there instead of being planted here.

You go on, "Speedy paid close attention anyway, because it wasn't long before his own tomatoes started popping up.

Regular fertilization is the ticket. I never touched one myself, but I took several up to Coke's place, sometime after he and Flippy moved from Center Street."

"You mean Mr. Haas down the hallway?" He points back with his thumb.

"That's not Coke down there, whatever's left in that room, that ain't Coke."

Roger's leaning his shoulder up against the doorframe now and crosses his arms.

"Told him, 'Coke, I brought some maters from the garden.' To this day, he doesn't like you calling him Coke, you know that, but he took the tomatoes. And don't you know, that first-class bullshitter tried to look excited. 'Now, Coke,' I told him, 'I want you to enjoy these. A special blend.'"

"Jack, you're awful," Roger says and laughs.

Makes you laugh out loud, too. "Other than being a son of a bitch," you tell him, "Coke was a pretty good worker. Matter of fact, he's largely responsible for my surviving the Golden Rod explosion. That's out by Five Points. They dug out the clay first, down lower. Then they took the number seven, when I come around, which is better coal, less sulfur, burns hotter. That's why they used it in glazing, in the sewer pipe. Of course, they say the best was from the big seam up around Youngstown and Sharon, Pennsylvania, but I don't know anything about that. Anyhow, we heard a terrible slam, then a whistling." You make your arms big and wide, and whistle. "I couldn't hear good to begin with. Then that shook the other eardrum. Took us both down to the ground, knocked us silly. I was fine." You shake your head. "That is to say, I wasn't dead. Found my way out of a ventilation shaft. One mother—this is true—lost several sons, like Mrs. Leotta years back. You ever heard of them mothers who lost all their boys in the world wars? Well, buddy, these was wars. They timbered the walls, and me and Coke dragged several men out, but two of them was dead already. I remember Shorty Martone's face was blowed half-off, but he was breathing yet. There was a picture of me and Coke in the paper. MIRACLE WORKERS, it said. SERVANTS OF GOD, they called us."

"Wow. And then you rewarded him with those tomatoes years later, huh?" Roger asks.

"You better believe it. Coke told me, 'Hell, those are some of the best damn tomatoes we've had in years.'"

Cancer's what's getting Coke in the end. Started in the colon, spread everywhere.

"No two ways about it," you say, "Speedy was good before he got ripped up."

Roger says the same thing over again: "Speedy sounds like he was a good dog, Jack."

"Speedy died late in the wintertime. Poor little devil. It had to have been two or three years back when I heard that whining off underneath the pines me and my cousin, Moon, planted there in '56. Speedy was breathing heavy-like. His insides hanging out. Blood running down his jaw, making his white belly pink." The words are hard coming out now, and you're sort of removed, listening to yourself talk it out. You take off your glasses and set them on the stand next to your chair. "That bastard brutalized Speedy," you say.

Roger comes and sits down next to you again, puts his hand towards the back of your chair, but rests it on the windowsill behind.

"Went in and got the .45 pistol Papa had found in Skunk Hollow when I was a kid. One he'd given me to shoot squirrel with Peaches. I walked to the old Salvadori family home. Salvadoris, you see, built a big house sometime after the War. One of the boys, one of Vic's grandsons, was cutting his mother's front lawn. 'Salvadori,' I said, handed over Papa's pistol, 'go put a bullet in Speedy, would you?'" You take your handkerchief from your back pocket and blow out each nostril, wipe your face.

Roger's looking down at your hands now.

You look up and tell him, "I don't ever remember not being able to shoot a dog."

Roger keeps his hand there, sits with you awhile, and lets you fall asleep first before he gets up and goes.

This Is What You Come to a Doughnut Shop For

Willy Jr. comes by Mercy about every other Saturday to take you out for an hour or so, to drive, to stop in Taylor's, the last doughnut shop in town, off of Water Street. He gets you in your chair, gets you your hat, and wheels you out to the front.

He has his Chevy Impala, a big automobile, pulled right up to the main entryway. He moves you and your chair through automatic doors, parks you, picks you up from the front, under your arms, and scoots you into the passenger's seat, your faces nearly touching, talking all the while about this and that, the coffee and tobacco from his breath spitting at you in droplets with each consonant. He lifts your legs up and in last. The boys used to come along with him, when you first got here, but anymore they stay home, or are playing ball, or riding their dirt bikes, or shooting guns, or something else. You get to watch Willy Jr. in the side mirror fold your wheelchair into itself and load it into the trunk. He tells you it's a big trunk. It must be, but it still takes him several slams to get it shut.

You never go far, but sometimes he takes you the long way, out along the Stillwater Creek, past the post office, which, he's told you, is down to four hours a day at the window. All the carriers have been moved to Uhrichsville, which covers just about everywhere at this end of the county anymore. Along the back road to Midvale, County Road 63, old Route 1, there are run-down homes with rusted-out burn barrels and stacks of used tires. You can see St. Theresa's new cemetery off to the east, probably eighty years new. This is where you'll pass when traveling north. The old cemetery, called Calvary Hill, sat up off Route 800, where, when passing, your mother taught you to cross yourself and pray to the Mother of God for all the lost souls, the ones dead in the ground, the ones waiting in Purgatory, the ones you'd wished were still living and walking, the ones who'd died in the 1918 flu and you'd never met. This is where Papa lay, an empty plot next to him waiting on Mama. She finally got there in '70s sometime. You're all in it together, those past and those left: *Pray for us sinners, now and at the hour of death*. In town, the church is red-bricked from the ground up with a grotto with the Virgin Mary sitting off to the left. It's a humble enough church, not extravagant, not hiding anything. You pass it, in a car, on foot, you cross yourself still. Anywhere there's a tabernacle with the blood and the body, you cross yourself, even if you don't say the full prayers, or confess your sins, or kneel down to chant or to sing, or believe in *any* of it. Old habits are hard to break.

Long ago, you rejected the dogma, any dogma, any orthodoxy, outside of the United Mineworkers of America, outside of John L. Lewis' advocacy for people like yours just asking for slim crusts of bread. But you think about Mary, the Mother of God, when driving out Route 800, or towards Midvale, or out of Dover towards Sugarcreek, or up the steep coal hills of Mineral City—anywhere the foreign and Catholic are buried. You think of the mother who lost her son and all the mothers around here who lost their sons. You ought to chant that Hail Mary out of your-self, towards whatever's out there, asking whatever there is to welcome warmly the free-floating souls of everyone you ever met and never met, for dead miners and dead family, for those four little children who got burned alive in the big farmhouse out at Barnhill. They rest in the new cemetery, along the back road to Midvale, buried all together—where you'll be buried soon enough, where Willy Sr. waits on Helen—their pictures carved into the headstone. That was Willy Jr.'s doing, of course, those engravings. Anyway, if there is a gentle woman up there, anywhere, you hope all these dead are enveloped in her quiet light.

* * *

By the time you get to Taylor's, everything's mostly picked over, fishermen getting up early to hit Clendenning Lake or the Stillwater. There used to be doughnut shops everywhere, all over town, open all night some of them. The old kind of doughnuts, lots of yeast, lots of sugar. DONUTS-COFFEE they used to say along the outside, or something like that. You used to post up and have a couple or three doughnuts, cup of coffee, and a cigarette or two. But that's not really what you ever came to a doughnut shop for.

Most of them closed down and now only Taylor's remains. This was started by Jooney, the old man, years ago, just after the War. If anyone had seen Jooney in his undershirt, no sleeves, sweat splish-splashing into the doughnut oil, they'd probably never have eaten any of his doughnuts. Taylor the boy is past 70, and you rarely see him there, home by six or seven o'clock most mornings. He's tall, sandy-haired, crippled up, his hands mangled something awful, a whole life spent rolling dough. Looks your age rather than his own. His mother went to school with Helen and could've finished high school if not for her son.

Inside are six barstools, a dozen or so booths, a loud waitress—Taylor's sister, Junebug, maybe 60—and several others, middle-aged, who've all been there forever, a rack of cookies and birthday cakes and small pies, a guy who fills out crosswords with a pencil stuck between his teeth because he can't use his arms. Taylor's sister is hollering at some old railroader about politics, it seems, and he's hollering back, and she starts pitching doughnut holes at him. He starts laughing like a little kid and crossing both his arms up in front of his face knocking his own hat off his head. "To hell with you today," she tells him. Taylor's fired her, his sister, three times that you know of, and by popular demand, she's back.

You like to order a whole bag of day-olds when you come in. Why not? You have all your teeth. This isn't like some McDonald's dollar menu, what the boys liked to go get when they came with their dad, the assortment of cheap things meant for the quick, the instant. These sweets are quick and instant still, sure, but not for the sake of being so.

The rolls and coffee are never more than four or five bucks, and Willy tells you to keep your wallet in your pocket. You stay in your chair when you come in, Willy rolling you past the big glass cases of deep-fried sweets. You point, going past, and say, "Man alive, would you look at the size of those?" Willy posts you up at the end of the counter, between that and the kitchen. He goes and looks in the display case, pointing out one to one of the help. Willy worked as a short-order cook when he was a teenager and acts at home in a place like this. He sits on the last barstool next to you. You look up and Junebug has calmed herself. You motion over to the big bags of day-olds, ask for one with apple fritters, and she says, "Must be hungry, Mr. August."

"Damn straight," you tell her.

"I know that's right," she says. "Where you two coming from today?"

"The deepmines."

Junebug laughs. "Oh, I've been there, yes I've been there. Been ten years probably, but I've been to those bad places."

Your doughnuts are brought over, along with small, round white plates, the coffee in brown mugs. Junebug says, "You know, last time I was in trouble? My daughter and I took her kids in her Jeep. Ten years ago, they were probably five and ten. You know the weather was like this out, and we slid and overturned, went right in the middle of the highway, sideways."

Willy Jr. says something like, "No kidding," while shoving half a maple cream stick in his mouth like it's going out of style. They wouldn't be allowed to call those doughnuts, if you had anything to say about it.

"Right over," she says. "She didn't have no tread on her tires. Had I known, I'd never have gotten in. Anyway, two men pulled off to the side and my daughter wanted help from them. I said hell no, but she insisted. So, you know that's when I still carried my pistol. I took it out of my coat pocket and said, 'Okay, they can help, but they trying anything, I'm shooting them both in the heart.'"

She refills your coffee. Everybody in the place is laughing and shaking their heads. When Junebug's talking, she's holding court, and she knows it.

"Have to shoot anybody in the heart?" you ask.

"Not them," she says. "They behaved themselves. People are good if you let them be."

This is what you come to a doughnut shop for.

* * *

You want to stay awhile longer, but she walks off and Willy says he can't linger on for too long today. Go ahead and eat your doughnuts, though, he says.

"No, no," you tell him. "Let's get moving."

Junebug's wiping off her hands and tells you she'll fix you both sandwiches for the way home. Willy brushes her off, but it'll only take a minute, she says. You can eat them back at the home, she says. "Isley's chip-chop, Pittsburgh-style."

"Ok," Willy says, "I'll come back."

"You okay with the relish, Mr. August? Cheese?" she asks.

"Sure, sure," you say.

"Sure you want the cheese, Uncle Jack?" Willy asks.

"Hell yes," you say.

He pushes you out to the Chevy, gets you loaded in, and hands you your bag of sweets, says he'll go get the sandwiches. He'll be right back, he says. You are parallel parked in front of Taylor's and figure you'll eat your fritter here in the car and save a cinnamon roll, covered in sugar glaze, for your roommate, Carl, back at Mercy. In front of you is a Subaru Outback, white. You'd have never seen these around here a few years ago. Cousin Moon used to talk about Subaru crushing any hope for the union over in Indiana. Your cousin had never been to Gary, or wherever it was, of course, but subscribed to literature about all of it. The vehicle has three bumper stickers. The first says KEEP ALASKA WILD. The second is a fish, like some of the help at Mercy have on their bracelets and shirts and probably vehicles, too, except it has feet and says DARWIN in the middle. You don't know too much about modern culture, but you do have a television set and know enough to know that this is what goes for being clever according to someone somewhere. The last sticker simply advertises Triple-A. Across the other side of the street, facing you, caddy-corner really, is a small sports utility vehicle. A Jeep? It doesn't look like any Jeep you ever saw, but it must be one. It has USMC in big letters on the driver's side rear window in a round white circle, outlined in black, and says—you figure—I SERVED underneath. You've seen those same ones before. Faded yellow ribbons are around it, too. Good thing they're still having wars. What else would they do with all those bumper stickers?

The car as the proclamation, as the expression of self. The car as the billboard, the tattoo. The car as a long reach for meaning after the steel leaves, and the railroads quit running, and they stop digging coal and clay around here. What's left for anyone anymore except to try to hold onto to some made-up identity, one you can buy at a shopping mall, one you can spell out on a small sign and stick onto your automobile? One that doesn't require getting on a ship and crossing the Atlantic and digging in deepmines.

At the stop light, waiting to get going, is a red pickup, a Chevy. It's worn out and run down, shaking and chug-a-lugging. There are a couple faded stickers even on it, on the windshield of it, but you can't tell what they are. National Rifle Association, maybe? Something for the local Mustang football team? Some declaration of Chevy's prowess over Ford, this old half-ton, hanging on, testament enough itself? Who knows?

A couple years back, one of the oldtimers from the South Side told you he saw a pickup parked at Argento's grocery with this hand-painted along the side: NEVER TRUST A PREACHER WITH A BONER. Hand-painted. Now, that tells a story. Willy thought it came from some rock and roll song, but regardless, that's a cautionary tale. That took time. That took love for one's fellow man. That's not a cheap-shit, half-assed bumper sticker that you can toss out or not, what's the difference. That's something worth saying.

"Here you go, Uncle Jackie," Willy Jr. says, getting back in the car and handing you a Styrofoam box. "Couple sandwiches. It'll be good for supper later. That Junebug's a livewire, ain't she?"

They can say what they want to about old Junebug Taylor, but she doesn't need some bumper sticker to know who she is. She's as true and honest as that hand-painted warning about preachers with boners.

"Might as well eat them doughnuts now, Uncle Jackie," he tells you. "Don't wait until they're two days old."

You manage to get the bag undone with your middle and ring fingers, rest a roll on your lap, and start bouncing your lips up and down in small breaths as Willy starts the engine. Bless us, oh Lord.

LAST RITES

Life Everlasting

You don't know what's taking so long in the kitchen. They brought Mama in to Mercy today and gave her an apron and a minestro and corn meal and boter and formag and a pot and a pan and they stood her over the stua and they're letting her fix up a whole lot of polenta for the whole staff here, who is organizing somebody said, so you ought to get that boza the janitor spits in and keep it close to your chest, hidden under your blanket, in case you need to bust some goddamn strikebreakers over the head with it.

Years ago, when the clay workers were negotiating, you remember them complaining about on-site bricklayers— people like Carl—getting higher wages than them, better pensions, and you told them it wasn't how much the bricklayers *were* getting paid, it was how much they *weren't* getting paid, goddamnit, and you don't know how long that strike is going to last, but if you can get your legs back underneath you and they can get a contract, you can get back to work, you figure. And if you can get back to work, you figure, you can buy a garnet necklace for Mama, and some zugatoli for the popi, and Lena her wedding dress, and that Cutlass Supreme the Salvadori boy is selling at his mother's house

163

and you can teach Willy Jr. to drive it since your cugna's dead and there's nobody else going to teach him to drive a manual shift, especially with wet nef coming down, finally starting to stick and piling up. You tell nobody in particular, "Von a ciasa." You try to say it louder: "Von a ciasa."

And there's cerf track right up to your window, some doe with lots of white around her eyes, her spotted fawn tight to her side, and they're eating at a feeder somebody like Roger probably put out there, and the doe surely isn't thinking a thing about bow season or gun season or muzzleloaders, since all she's thinking of is looking after her sweet child, getting that baby its corn, right up here at your window, right up here at this old folks' home.

How in hell did you get here?

And wouldn't you know, there he is a hundred yards away, that little son of a bitch, old Speedy. His head's barely above the snow, looking back at you. And you hope to God Speedy doesn't sniff up on that mother cerf and start on a chase. You don't have it in you to deer-break Speedy, but those deer are safe with you, with old Giacomo with nothing to do but look right back at them, the last Agostini standing. They brought the deer into Ohio and are getting your people out. You wipe your mouth off with the corner of your blanket, wipe away the whipping cream they put on top of the jello here.

You must've been ten years old when you would steal fruit and cream pies from Mrs. Salvadori's windowsill, and Lena says, looking back, Flora knew you would do that, set those apple-and-nut and black-bottom custard pies out since she knew you and Coke were waiting, and Flora would call you Giaco the diavolo, and she'd put out another the next Sunday, too.

That must be Mama now, rubbing the sides of your shoulders, so you take off your capel since you're inside and should've done it before and rest it on your lap, and you ask her when Moon and Norman are coming by and she isn't saying a thing back to you, ask her when the service for Zia Giusseppina is, and she isn't saying a thing back to you, ask her what she needs from Argento's, and she isn't saying a thing back to you, ask her if you can keep any of the litter Peaches had, and she isn't saying a thing back to you, and she's holding some rope or rosary or something and so you start saying it all with her: "Pere nost, che t'ies en ciel, al sie santifiché ti inom."

Someone you don't know gives you a kiss on the cheek and holds your head close and you ask, "Come te clames po?" and she keeps saying some name over and over back to you and pats your knee, saying "fradel," and holds your head tighter to hers, and she smells like Youth-Dew bath oil, and a nun comes and starts wheeling you away from the window, from the mother deer and her fawn, from Speedy. And maybe if that sister knew you were from the same family tree as Padre Chino she'd pay you some respect, and you try to holler out the rest—for Mama to hear, not for this nun—but it only comes out as a whisper, like you're talking in your sleep: "Al vegne ti regn, sia fata tia volonté, coche en ciel enscì en tera."

Last Rites

Her brother's bed had cost him one-hundred and fifty dollars a day, and there's no doubt they'd peel the rosary ring from his finger in the end, too, if they could get away with it. Forget the Virgin Mother, Helen thinks, forget the Son of God. This is grade-A, American capitalism, the ownership society, and Jackie isn't about to make it out of this intensive care unit owning any goddamn thing, even the beaded steel stretched around the bent, meaty hooks on his left hand. He owned his home. He owned his dogs. He owned dump truck after dump truck. He owned his twelve-gauge shotguns and the .45 from Papa. He owned the Val di Non plate from Mama, like the one Helen brought to Mercy in these last days, the one she placed on his shelf next to the family picture, the one the help must have misplaced. He's owned these things, paid for in cash or acquired from love, but not his long death. This is Uncle Sam's. Bury him under a heap of number six coal, why don't they?

And here she is, getting up and refilling the pink plastic pitcher of water that sits on a hospital tray in front of her family, waiting for a priest her son's age to come free her brother from sin.

Jackie's oxygen tank hooks through his nostrils and pumps, and it will longer than needed. The way these things work, they'll pump until someone shuts them off. Nothing humane about it. Just automatic, mechanical ventilation.

At least the mine explosions crushed Papa and Zio all at once, the full humans smashed, bones and all, like silverfish in a kitchen corner, not left to wither away into nothing, hanging on by some torture device.

Too bad this place weren't a coal mine, she figures. If only those tubes on the tank would break, crack right open, and fill the room. Firedamp. Stinkdamp. Afterdamp. If only Willy Jr. would still smoke Camels instead of wearing a patch, he could strike a match. If only everyone in the room would tumble to the ground when it all went up. If only her son and his wife would catch fire, her grandsons get smashed against the wall by a slab of black rock, then her big brother would leap from the bed. He'd save them all. He'd pry the boys free, carry them over each shoulder. He'd drag Willy Jr. and Susan out, too, haul them to the fresh snow. He could live and they could live and he could toss the goddamn rosary ring back in the flames that would fill the intensive care unit and they'd all watch the smoke tear through Mercy Hospital, the fires melting the blackened snows on the asphalt outside. They could all speak Nones language while tracing the warm gray waters as they'd seep into the creek bed just beyond the hospital.

*　*　*

The only explosion is that of Susan's hysterical sobs. The mother of Helen's grandchildren, noticeably heavier than ever now, wails as her husband puts his small hands on her back. She has big, teased hair, a Christmas sweater, and she claws at Jackie's legs. She looks god-awful and has made her boys read Bible passages out loud, two teenagers muttering in robotic cadence. But Helen's grandsons mostly drink water from Dixie cups nearby and watch their shoestrings. The soft pudginess these boys have grown into has nothing to do with adolescence, and everything to do with their American parents. Willy Jr.'s family is a far cry from Tyrol, a far cry from Ellis Island, a far cry from the old Rosemarie mine. And Susan has seldom been to the Mercy Retirement Community in the several years that Jackie has spent here. She sure showed up now, though, just in time for him to die. What if all his money was gone? What if he never did get that oil lease? Would he be so venerated?

* * *

The last time Helen really spoke to her brother was weeks ago. She'd been folding his flannel shirts and making sure that his blankets were where they were supposed to be, in his closest. He had woken up and began moving in his wheel-chair just barely with his feet, inching across the room to steal candy from Carl's top drawer while the old bricklayer slept. She saw this and chastised him in a mixture of their language and American English. He took candy anyway and she began to recount a story of Theodore Reynolds, the grandson of the Rosemarie and Golden Rod mine owners, who'd built a several-million-dollar home on Cowboy Hill. He'd gone to high school with Willy Jr., she reminded Jackie, and to college somewhere afterwards. He went to several, she'd heard. He'd been what you'd call a full-time student, and after, he tore down the family estate to build a big, empty, miserable mansion.

She saw the inside of it once when her daughter-in-law took her on a Christmastime tour of homes uptown. Susan would finger the garland and gaze at the many Christmas trees and continually remark to Helen, "Isn't this just wonderful?"

Theodore Reynolds had greeted visitors as they entered, Helen recalled. He looked just like a Reynolds: tall, over six feet, lean, small glasses magnifying brown eyes, and short slicked hair. He shook their hands, and he asked Helen who she was. She told him and accepted his extended hand, it no firmer than a dead perch. He smiled like a weathergirl or a kitchenware salesman might and moved on to greet the next visitor. The only other detail that stuck with Helen from that day, she told Jackie, was her daughter-in-law's insistence as they walked that the workers in the warehouse where Susan had been a secretary, workers who had failed to organize the previous year and to whom she'd passed out modest Christmas hams for bonuses, were "lazy, entitled half-assers." Since the last layoffs, Helen reminded her brother, Susan has been collecting unemployment again.

There was big furniture, gadgets, crystal chandeliers, children's toys that looked like space-aged machines, and spiraling staircases, but there wasn't a whole lot of love in that place. How much it must be to heat a home like that, she wondered, and didn't care if she ever saw it again. But every year for the better part of the last decade, *The Daily Recorder* had shown the newest Christmas decorations Mrs. Reynolds had placed in, on, and around the house.

Anyway, the Reynolds boy hanged himself. She'd just read the short obituary on the back page of the front section that morning. Died unexpectedly is all it said. And this Christmas, see if there'd be any pictures of lights, mangers, or wreath-laden pillars in *The Recorder*. Susan, who loved rich people's gossip even more than rich people's homes, telephoned to tell her mother-in-law there were no pills swallowed, no guns fired, no jump to the base of the cliff on which his home sat, a good hundred feet down from the top of Theodore Reynolds' stucco monstrosity. Apparently, there was no note either. Instead, Susan told her that he hanged himself in the cellar and then explained the lewd details about what some are saying led to it, some saying he was found in the nude. Susan had seen Mrs. Reynolds at Argento's just that week buying half a pound of ham salad, she'd said. A rich woman buying ham salad *just like* Susan!

Helen didn't tell Jackie, but she imagined Mrs. Reynolds making small sandwiches for her little boy and girl with the crusts removed and cut into triangles while her husband's broken neck swung tight in a noose from an I-beam below.

After Helen got through the whole story, Jackie unwrapped the foil and paper on a chocolate bar and laughed a hard, "Ha!" He put half the bar in his mouth and stopped his wheelchair in the middle of the freshly mopped floor. He pulled his glasses from his face and his wrinkles stretched and smoothed. His grin went from one side to the other; his eyes squinted and just a slice of blue peered out. He fiddled with the candy more, but his stare went to some other place, far past the sterile tile and flowered wallpaper of the nursing home. It was as if they were scanning over everything that ever happened in the last ninety years. Helen wondered at whom or what her brother was smiling so still and wide-eyed, like some kind of magnificent statue made of Vatican marble.

"How do you like that?" he finally said, mostly to himself, and coughed a few more laughs. It was the kind of molten laughter that empties into a room, stiffens up, and holds everything in place.

Helen admitted she'd only read about half of the piece in the paper and started to dust the dresser top, not her job but per her routine. She had seen Jackie most days in the weeks since, but he never said much of anything back to her.

And now, here they are.

Jackie's chest moves up and down, his head cocked back. One of the nurses must have situated him like that. Helen pushes the pillow in more behind his head. His eyes squeeze hard and shut, like there is no prying them. The air blowing into him is forced. It's cold in the hospital, so Helen adjusts Jackie's blanket just a little here and there, even though his body doesn't move except his chest. Really, there is nothing much she can do now, but any comfort she can give, she owes him.

Put it this way: Jackie is her brother, as much a brother as any brother in any family that has ever been. Heavens, yes. In the summertime when she was six, he taught her to swim by launching her into a muddy creek. Her head nearly stuck in the mud, she remembers, but as she came up, the chalky waters burning deep in her nose, she saw Jackie grinning, knees bent at the edge, and while she was full of righteous indignation to be sure, she was safe, too. He was ornery as hell, but good as bread. In the early fall, he'd turn his own hands and clothes ink black, picking buckets full of walnuts and peeling away the hulls, spreading them to dry over old blankets, and shelling them with a ball-peen hammer, just because she liked walnuts.

And when she was grown and married, he'd transplanted white spruces, rose of Sharon, crabapples, and any other shrub, tree, or bush Helen mentioned she'd like at her home. That's where all the silver maples come from, the ones they're clearing for drilling. And in the bad years, Jackie handed over five-thousand dollars cash when Willy Sr.'s sugar got out of control and they started cutting pieces of him off. Jackie was the brother who hauled moonshine while she read books when they were young. In school, his clothes were ragged; hers, spotless. He'd left St. Theresa's during junior high, and she graduated with a high school diploma. He was a miracle in her life, and now he's here. That's the real sin.

* * *

Finally, Father Ralph comes in to give the final sacrament a Catholic gets. He speaks with the family just briefly and sweetly smiles like he's not there to see a dying man. He doesn't remove his scarf or jacket, and pats Helen's bent shoulders as she lifts her head to make eye contact. He then turns to Jackie, takes him in a moment, and generally seems good at his job, anointing the sick.

Jackie will be dead before long, like her husband years back, like Mama and Papa before that, like the Reynolds boy, like Jesus Christ. It'd have been better in a coal mine like Papa or from a noose like the Reynolds boy, better still on a cross, a martyr for something.

For what?

Just the same, they'll all be square.

Father begins the prayers and by the time he crosses olive oil on Jackie's forehead, saying, "May the Lord who frees you from sin save you and raise you up," while her big brother's chest expands and contracts, Helen has stopped paying attention.

Acknowledgments

Several of the stories in this collection first appeared in earlier forms in the following publications: *The Showcase*, *Italian America*, and *The Blotter Magazine*. "Effetto Montagna," which first appeared in *The Showcase* in July 2022, was generously nominated for a Pushcart prize by one of Pushcart's Contributing Editors. An earlier version of the full collection titled *Dago Red* was previously named a Finalist for Big Fiction's Knickerbocker Prize and a Finalist at Black Hill Press, and was included on a longlist for Brickhouse Books. Some material, as noted in particular stories, was obtained from the now-defunct New Philadelphia *Daily Times*. Meanwhile, the Tyrolean American magazine, *Filo*, was incredibly helpful with sorting out Nones dialect and introducing the author to the phrase, "effetto montagna."

The author's own great-grandparents—including Tyroleans, Sicilians, and Appalachian Americans who lived and worked in the coal mining regions of Eastern Ohio—must be acknowledged: Gennaro and Concetta De Monte (as well as Concetta's second husband, Luigi Argento), Giacomo and Recie DeBiasi, Erminio and Emilia Chini, and Harry and Lena Stanley. All four of his grandparents, too: Frank and Grace De Monte, and Philip and Dorothy Stanley. Also, a great-uncle: David Chini. It is through their stories that the author came to fully appreciate where his people are from.

Many thanks are owed to the fine staff at Cornerstone Press, too, including publisher Dr. Ross Tangedal, editorial director Brett Hill, managing editor Maria Scherer, and production editor Julia Kaufman. Throughout every stage of the publishing process, they proved to be incredibly professional, collaborative, and open-minded, making this all a thoroughly enjoyable experience.

Lastly, the author's wife, Leah, has offered much love and patience during the writing of this book, as well as cover art.